Life After Better Days

Pain. Past. Purpose.

Books Published by Anita 'Nina' Porter

Better Days

Life After Better Days

Pain. Past. Purpose.

By

Anita 'Nina' Porter

Published by Forever And A Day Publishing LLC.
Triangle, Virginia 22172

ISBN Paperback: 979-8-9988364-1-1

10 9 8 7 6 5 4 3 2 1

Printed in the United States of America

Letter To My Readers

Dear Readers,

    Faith means doing something when you don't feel like it. Being faithful is a test for a promotion. Faithfulness is about doing it when it gets hard. It's about doing it when you don't get the credit for it. I'm saying all this to say...

    Wow, I'm here again, writing about the major parts of my life to you. In hopes that I can grow and possibly help someone whose life was like mine or know someone who has dealt with anything they are about to read. My book is very detailed and real.

    I especially wanted to write *Life After Better Days* because I am a very private individual; I love my peace, and I love my happiness. I'm just an all-around concealed type of person. However, I know that sometimes it can be harmful to yourself when it's time to explain your life. It all runs together, whether it's days, weeks, months, or years later, of what you wanted to speak about. It can damage your way of thinking, so please find your go-to person and understand that I don't want you to live that life. I have to say that to myself daily because what

    I speak on, and I'm still working on it to this day. Now, after 36 years, I release my emotions through writing. I have a few go-to people that I can confide in, but I only release what I think is necessary. I have also learned that you must watch what you share with certain individuals, because they will use it against you. So, be cautious!

Don't be a prisoner of your own mind, but release what you think is needed, depending on the person. I also learned to approach people who can help with my situation without causing harm. I love open topics. I also appreciate it when someone shares their narrative if they were in that predicament. Some people don't like it because they feel like the spotlight should be on them at the time. I honestly don't look at it that way.

I feel as though we could help each other knock two birds out with one stone. It's an amazing feeling to receive another person's perspective on things and to also share your thoughts with them. Use that platform, whether it's your mother, friend, spouse, or someone else you're venting to; don't be afraid to be vulnerable. So, I say this to my readers before reading my book: "THERE ARE SOME GOOD PEOPLE OUT HERE IN THIS WORLD." You must set apart the real from the fake. Moving forward in my message to you, having faith without A PURPOSE, is a dead situation. You can't have faith without a purpose; you'll lose every time.

Exercise your mind, train yourself for anything to happen, and still live a positive life. Stand on what you believe and never second-guess any decisions you make in life. Whatever you decide, STAND ON IT with both feet. Never be fearful of what's going to happen; just make sure it's right for you. Don't live life for anyone else; live for you. Oh, and stand up straight, look people in the eyes — that means you're serious.

Even in pain, stand strong and grow through what you go through. My ending message to my readers is this: Keep in mind that it's a clock ticking that we can't see. So, enjoy life; don't live in the darkness of your mind. Shed some light on yourself, protect your feelings, but have some feelings to spare, just enough not to be played with. YOUR STORY is your story, whether you make a journal diary or a book. Tell it and encourage, inspire, or motivate someone. TRUST ME, people are watching, so why not tell my *LIFE AFTER BETTER DAYS*?

Especially if you lived in the shadows like me, being misunderstood, embarrassed, happy, sad, disgusted, vulnerable, excited, and the list goes on.

Remember, life goes on but live it while you're alive.

While reading *Life After Betters Days...* I would like for you to read it in two parts the RAW version and then the polished version. Doing that gives you the adrenaline feeling and then the calmness of my reality. going from intense to refined is basically how my life is written and I'm not ashamed to say that but wanted to be honest with every reader reading the high lights of my life. Sit back and enjoy what I worked so hard on.

I love y'all!

Nina

↔

Writing this wasn't easy. Releasing these parts of me took guts. It took getting out of my own way. It took confronting the walls I built and finally admitting to my truth: I want to be heard. Not because I need attention, not because I want sympathy, but because I want freedom. The kind of freedom that comes when you finally lay your story down and say, "I lived it. I survived it. And I'm still here."

There were many moments I felt like shutting this book down, deleting everything, and just keeping it all inside like I always have. But something deep inside told me that silence won't serve me anymore. Not now. Not when I know my words could be what helps somebody get through their own version of hell.

I know pain intimately. I know what it's like to sit in a room full of people and still feel alone. I know what it's like to laugh, to smile, to post, and still be dying inside. So, I'm not writing this as some expert. I'm writing this as a woman who is still healing, still learning, still showing up every day, trying to figure out what joy even looks like now.

I was always the one who held it all together, who people came to, and the one who smiled through heartbreak and loss. The one who loved deeply even when it wasn't returned. But writing taught me I don't have to carry everything anymore. Not every memory. Not every scar. Not every secret.

Do you ever get tired of wearing the *strong friend* badge? I did. That's when I knew I had to start unpacking.

This book is a piece of that unpacking. It's for the girl I used to be. It's for the mother I became. It's for the woman I'm still growing into. And it's for YOU — whoever you are, wherever you are — who needs a reminder that you are not crazy, not broken, not too far gone. You're just evolving.

So, cry when you need to. Close the book if it gets too heavy. Come back to it when your heart feels ready. But don't give up on your story.

We don't get to rewrite the past, but we do get to reclaim it. And baby, this is me doing exactly that.

Dedication

I often wondered where life would take me. To be honest, it has taken me on a rollercoaster ride, I mean, for real, a fast one. But I have a few people I want to thank.

Now, this is my second book, and in the 5 years since *Better Days*, I've had some awesome people by my side. I want to thank God, first. People often don't realize that whoever you pray to is listening. He has gotten me through so much; I have been through so much. When I needed to be picked up and walked through in my journey, I knew I had God to stand by my side. I'm forever grateful that even when I couldn't find myself, God knew who I was. He knew I was destined to be unique and great and gave me the strength to keep stepping and look at ya' girl I'M STEPPING. Thank You, God.

Next, I would like to thank my beautiful mother, Leslie. She is probably one of the strongest women I know. Mom, I want to thank you for giving me life when you knew the odds weren't in your favor with my father. You didn't care. You gave me life and you figured it out. Thank you for believing in me even when I didn't believe in myself. Whenever I call you for advice, you give it to me, whether I like it or not. YOU GIVE IT. Where would I honestly be without you? You're so beautiful inside and out.

Mommy, you are everything. From the way you sacrificed, to the way you never gave up on me even when I gave up on myself

— I will always owe you the deepest kind of love. You didn't have all the answers, but you had heart, and you taught me what it means to be a real woman. You showed me what survival looks like with your chin high and your back straight, even when your soul was tired. I'm forever appreciative of the love I have for you. I can't even explain it in words. I will just try to show you every day. Mommy, you did so well raising six children. WEAR your crown gracefully.

Next, I would like to thank my siblings Lil Dante, Vanessa, Donisha, Dominic, Danielle, Danyette, and Dontel. Y'all are a piece of me. All of us are different. All of us have our own battles. But together... we are solid! We've laughed together, cried together, fallen out, made up, and still came back home to each other. That's love. That's blood. That's us. We are a unit, we are strong, we are fighters, we are warriors, we are weak, we are strong, we stick together, WE got this even when we feel like we don't have it, and WE HAVE EACH OTHER.

To the people who held me when I couldn't hold myself — this is for you. You may never know how your presence, your words, or your belief in me helped pull me out of some of the darkest places I've ever been.

To my babies — even though I'll thank you again later, I want to say this now: You are the reason I breathe differently. The reason I stay alive when I want to give up. You gave me purpose when the world was trying to strip it from me. Every word in this book carries a piece of the love I feel for you.

Lastly, I want to thank all my supporters, whether they were for or against me. Yes, I said it! The good ones supported me and critiqued my first book, and I loved it. I even took in what I needed to fix, and I never felt any type of way. I used that and executed it. For the quiet ones who never needed credit, I see you. I feel your prayers. I hear your encouragement even when you don't say a word. And yes, even the critics - you helped sharpen me. And to every person who thought I wouldn't make it, this book is my way of saying I did.

Wait, wait, hold up. I also want to thank the ones who were placed in my life, some for a reason, a season, and a lifetime. I won't name names but thank you!!! Now that I have thanked everyone, I want you to enjoy *Life After Better Days*.

Acknowledgments

These acknowledgments come from deep down in my heart. My brother Dom has been my backbone, even with being incarcerated.

I remember mailing him *Better Days*, and he said, "Soulja Sis, hmm.., I like it, but I want you to go harder."

Life After Better Days has been written for years; it's essentially 'My Pain, Past, and Purpose.' However, I was too afraid for it to be released. But after speaking with him, that confirmation hit me at a rapid speed, and I've been on it ever since.

His words, and I quote, "Soulja Sis, fuck that, let's hear your story! Stop playing with me. It's your story, and no one else can tell it like you. Plus, why would you want anyone to bend and fabricate your life? Tell it how it is, and we don't care who doesn't like it. LET'S GET IT!"

So, with that being said, welcome to my world of *Life After Better Days* (Pain, Past, and Purpose). Writing a book like this was not easy. It takes a lot out of you emotionally, mentally, and even spiritually. But one thing I've learned is that healing is not always quiet. Sometimes it manifests in the form of storytelling, and this is my story, told in the way I lived it, felt it, and survived it.

To my Father God, thank You. Thank You for loving me in ways I couldn't always see and holding me in seasons I didn't think I'd survive. I've questioned You. I've been mad at You. But I always knew You were there. You never left me. Even when I turned my back. Even when I got too weak to pray. And for that, I honor You first.

To my family, my heart is with y'all. Every name mentioned, every story shared, every tear that came from a childhood memory — it's all here, wrapped in these pages. We didn't always have the perfect situation, but we had love. We had grit. We had something that couldn't be broken, not even when life tried to shake us.

To my mother, Leslie — you deserve an entire book of your own, but I tried to honor you on every page. Your strength is stitched into my backbone. Your love taught me resilience. And even on your worst day, you were still my hero. I love you more than words will ever say.

To my father, I will carry you with me. But your name lives in me. I honor your memory with this book. You mattered to me. You still do. And if you can see me from where you are, in heaven, I hope you're proud. This is your daughter rising.

To every friend who became family, thank you. You listened to me vent. You checked in when I got quiet. You reminded me who I was when I almost forgot. Whether we talk every day or not, I hold those moments with love. And to the ones who faded away, I still thank you. Some lessons had to come through loss.

To my readers, wow! The fact that you even picked up this book means the world to me. Whether you're reading it to understand me or to understand yourself better, I want to say thank you. You are the reason I didn't give up on telling my truth. If something I wrote helps you heal, then every tear I cried writing this was worth it.

Lastly, to ME. I must thank myself. For showing up. For staying the course. For pushing through breakdowns, heartbreaks, sleepless nights, and moments of deep self-doubt. Nina, you did that. You came back stronger. You kept your promise to your younger self. You told the story that was buried inside your bones. And now look, you're free. This book is for the warrior in me and the one in you.

Welcome to Life After Better Days

This isn't just a book. It's a map — a raw, unfiltered map — of my life's journey through pain, struggle, growth, and ultimately, purpose. When I first started writing, I wasn't sure what I was creating. I just knew I had to get my story out. Because sometimes the only way to heal is to shine a light on the parts of your life you've been afraid to face.

I want you to know from the very beginning: this book is real. It's messy. It's honest. Sometimes it's hard to read. But it's also filled with hope.

Hope for anyone who feels stuck in their own past. Hope for anyone who wonders if they can ever break free from the chains of their pain. Hope for anyone who needs a reminder that the darkness won't last forever — that better days can come, but only after you're willing to fight for them.

I'm not perfect. I'm still learning every day how to stand in my truth, own my story, and walk with my head held high, even when the weight feels unbearable.

If you pick up this book, know that you're not alone. Whatever you're facing, I want you to hold onto this one thing: Your story matters. Your pain is valid. Your healing is possible.

So, let's take this journey together. Let's walk through the pain, look back at the past, and step into purpose. Because on the other side of the storm, there really are better days waiting.

Welcome to *Life After Better Days.*

— *Nina*

CONTENTS

Introduction

"You know me, I DON'T NEED NO INTRODUCTION to shit."

Naw, I'm just excited, y'all. It's been five long years since I became an author and publisher. I love what I do. I inspire motivation and just make people smile. Let me start by saying the world we live in can be beautiful, but it can also be cruel. You must somehow live through it day by day. I always was and still am an overthinker. I always wanted to know what the other planets were like, Mars, Jupiter, and shit. For real, I've been on Earth for 35 years, and sometimes life just isn't fair. We must take the good with the bad, whether we're happy or sad, and it can get overwhelming, but in the same breath, it teaches us.

I honestly love my life because I'm a very diverse person, so even when life isn't working for me, I make it work. I use my head and come up with a plan. I can't be defeated, my mind is strong, and I love that about myself. I have weak moments, but I turn everything I go through into a lesson, and I learn from it, even if it's multiple times of me going through it.

Life After Better Days is legit and the truest, solidest I can get. I deserve this platform, and as you read my story, I hope you understand that I have no intention of disrespecting or discrediting anyone. Take this as an assignment to learn a little, embarrass yourself, cut some people off, add and subtract your surroundings, and try to look at life differently, because I have been through a lot. I put my thoughts and pain into my pen, and I put it on paper and made another gold mine. After this, I may not write another book, so enjoy every moment. Be proud of me after you read my book, make some changes, and ultimately be proud of yourself for the change you want in your life. I love y'all!

PAIN

PAIN: Part I

That was the day I was born; a chocolate fat baby with big cheeks, beautiful, weighing 8 pounds 14 ounces. My mom was in so much pain; it was unbearable. As she screamed for me to come out, my aunt was there for support, and here, I finally came. Now that was just the good part.

My mom was young when she conceived me with my biological father, whom I never knew. Even growing up, I could never remember him being there for birthdays, Christmas, or any other special occasions. My mom never really talked about him, good or bad, so I always had that emptiness. I always wondered "Why," but I had my mom.

She was my idol. I admired her because she was incredibly beautiful to me. Her dark chocolate skin and a perfectly white smile were stunning. What I love about my mom is her presence, as well as her no-holds-barred approach. I was also blessed with my dad, and if you know me, you know my dad is Dante.

He met my mom when she was 8-9 months pregnant with me, and they've never gone anywhere since. To be quite honest, growing up, I always thought that was my biological father. It didn't matter about the color of me and him. What mattered the most was the love he showed me and my sister. I could remember my mother telling me the story of when I messed up dad's back because he carried me up a hill, and I was a chunky baby. Literally!

Now let's rewind it just a little bit. Before I was born, my mom had another child (who is my sister) so I always remember it being just me and my sister. We were like Frick and Frack. My mom used to dress us up the same way and we'd go to parties.

People would always say, "They look so cute, Leslie."

My sister and I were tight, but we had our moments, too! I could remember one time she cut my hair and made me drink medicine. We just did normal things with each other. We argued and fought, but for the most part, it was love. We were never apart, even when we had different friends and were three years apart. It was always Nish and Nina.

My mother was everything and more. We never saw her weak moments, and even if she was, none of her children observed it. I wrote a poem just for her, and here it is:

The Light

Mommy you are the light.

I often wonder how you found the energy to raise six children, and I ask that all the time?

You were our teacher, nurse, counselor, and so much more then and now; how did you do it all, Mommy?

Be our cook, disciplinary person, our protector, provider, and you pray for us daily?

I just can't comprehend. I see even when I was younger and a grown adult, it was everlasting love that would never end.

I thank you for it all, you are my light that'll never stop shining bright.

Love, **Nina**

↔

Pain has many faces. For me, it started the moment I took my first breath. My mother's pain was so intense, yet through that agony came I, a beautiful baby with big cheeks and a spirit that refused to be broken. But pain was already weaving through my family's story, long before I was born.

My biological father was a mystery, a shadow I never truly knew. I grew up with more questions than answers about him. Birthdays, holidays, any moments where a father might show up— he was absent. The silence about him from my mother created a space that echoed with the question, "Why wasn't he there?" That emptiness could have swallowed me whole, but my mom— she was my anchor, my safe harbor.

She was young and brave, carrying the weight of so many responsibilities with grace. Her beauty wasn't just skin deep— it was in her presence, her strength, and the way she never sugar-coated anything. She faced life head-on, and because of her, I learned what it meant to be resilient.

Then there was Dante— my dad, the man who stepped in when I needed him most. He met my mom late in her pregnancy, but he stayed. His love was a quiet force in my life. It never mattered that he wasn't my biological father because his heart was fully mine and my sister's.

Growing up, my sister and I were inseparable. We were partners in crime, best friends, and occasional rivals. Like any siblings, we had our battles— cut hair, forced medicine, petty fights— but always underneath it all, love held us together. Our bond was unbreakable, a constant reminder that no matter what came our way, we had each other.

My mother's strength was the foundation of our family. Though she carried burdens none of us fully understood, she never showed weakness in front of us. She was our teacher, nurse, counselor, and protector, all rolled into one. Her prayers were our shield, and her love was the light guiding us through the darkest days.

That poem I wrote for her is my tribute to the woman who gave me life, who held our family up when the world felt heavy. She is my light— steady, bright, and unwavering.

Those were the days... Now, let's fast forward to my sister and me. We never grew up with our fathers. I always wanted to ask my sister, 'Who is your dad?' because, although my mom, sister, and I were dark-skinned, my sister and I don't look alike. We never questioned it because of the love my mom and dad gave us. It took away the flesh of our fathers, but not the pain that we felt.

Growing up, like I said, we always had our mom. She never drank, smoked crack or cigarettes, but she did smoke weed. I could always remember her doing that to the point where we knew what it smelled like from afar, but despite her smoking weed, we were always taken care of... *Always*!

Growing up with two daughters in the late 80s and early 90s, smoking weed was good because so many people were doing crack. Crack was out in full effect, but nope, not my mom. I'm so glad she was a hard worker dedicated to what she did. I never knew my mother to be jobless. She always tried to make ends meet.

For a minute, it was just my sister and me, but then my little brother came. When I said that was the happiest day of our lives, it truly was. He was perfect! So now it was me, my sister, my little brother, my mom and my dad. We never had a bad childhood; it was just normal. We always had what we needed, and when we didn't, we eventually got it somehow.

In the process of growing up, my dad was dealing with his traumas. He drank a lot! I mean every day, but my dad was a hero to us. He was very overprotective, to say the least. He made sure we were fed and bathed. He'd used to walk us to school and taught us never to be afraid.

Looking back, as I got older, I think that was why he was the way he was, because he had no choice. He was deaf, so his voice was either muffled or very loud. My dad not only struggled with being an alcoholic, but also with his personal struggles, and it showed. I bet that had to be hard on him, having to step up and deal with two children because of the love he had for my mom. But he got the job done.

Those were the days!

Life had its ups and downs, but in those early years, my sister and I shared a childhood shaped more by love than by absence. We never grew up knowing our fathers in the way most kids do. Sometimes, I wondered about my sister's father— who he was, what he looked like— but those questions were swallowed up by the strength and affection of the people who raised us. The color of our skin or the lack of resemblance didn't matter.

What mattered was the love we received, the love that filled the empty spaces left by absent fathers. My mom was our rock. She never gave in to the temptations that trapped so many around her. No alcohol, no crack, no cigarettes— only weed, which she used sparingly and responsibly in those days. Despite that, she worked hard to keep a roof over our heads and food on the table. Watching her hustle and struggle instilled in me a deep respect for perseverance. She was always employed, always making ends meet, always there.

The late '80s and early '90s were a tough time in many neighborhoods. Crack cocaine was devastating communities, but not ours. My mom protected us from that chaos, steering clear of destruction and providing a safe space where love and dedication reigned. She was a hard worker, a fighter, and because of her, we had stability. Then came my little brother, the bundle of joy who made our family complete. I remember that day like it was yesterday. His arrival brought pure happiness, and suddenly, our little unit was bigger.

My dad was a complex man. His demons were real - battles with trauma and alcoholism shadowed his life, yet, he was our hero. Overprotective, fierce, and loving, he showed up every day.

His deafness shaped his world— his voice was loud, intense, and sometimes intimidating— but it was his way of being heard in a world that was often silent. I think some of that boldness rubbed off on me. I learned to speak loudly and clearly, to assert myself and demand to be heard.

The weight he carried wasn't easy. Balancing his addictions and personal battles while trying to be the man his family needed was a daily fight. But love for my mom and kids kept him going. Though he wasn't perfect, he got the job done in his own way.

Behind it all, my mom was the steady provider, the breadwinner, the backbone of the family. Her strength, determination, and love created a foundation that held us up through everything. She stayed working, so that left us with our dad. He taught us children a lot. He also didn't play any games. If you did something, he made you stand by what you did, including the punishment. My sister, brother, and I stayed in the corner, LOL! I just had to elaborate on that so y'all could understand and keep up. My dad was harder and still harder than a lot of men I know.

I definitely felt alone in many ways, though, because I was always a smart kid. I always knew that my dad wasn't my biological father because I was always told when my father's name was mentioned that I was his only child. Until this day, he is serving his time and has many more years to go.

The stories my mother told me about Chuckie were something I didn't care to hear, but I listened to them anyway. In reality, I wish I hadn't been introduced to him or even told he was my father, because I was okay with the dad I had. Of course, at this old age, I'm not mad at my mom. Still, for a long time, I hated the fact she even named me after a woman, Chuckie's mother, and I never even knew her. I HATE MY NAME. I was better off just not knowing anything. Still, hey, this is my story and it's part of me.

Growing up was cool. I still don't know who my dad was (in the flesh.)

Now my mom is on her 3rd child. Dom, the first child, my mom and dad had together, was my mother's first son. Prior to that my father had a son named Lil Dante who we loved as well. Myself and my sister Nish were happy to have our little brother around. (Proceed with "One day I found out my mom was pregnant again having twins.)

I could remember my mom coming home, and Nish (my older sister) was holding Danyette, while I was holding Danielle. They were baby dolls, and we adored them. We were always happy to hold them and kissing them was the best. Man, those were the days, but then we had some not-so-good days as well.

Now, in my last chapter, I told you all about my dad and his heavy drinking. Although he drank excessively, he lived up to his name for many years. Even to this day, he copes with alcohol. Well, he may have calmed down just a little because of age and health issues, but shit, growing up was hell living with someone who was broken. He didn't know how to deal with his childhood traumas, and we saw it as kids.

One night, I heard my mom crying badly and my dad yelling. He was angry as hell, and all of a sudden, I heard him beating her. I cried for my mom that night and put my pillow over my head so I couldn't hear it anymore. I don't even know if she knows I know this, but I don't forget anything. This continued for some time; nevertheless, my mom never showed weakness. NEVER!

You never know what your kids see or hear. My mom's kids weren't allowed to sit and listen to adults talk, but I wasn't stupid either. I knew she was getting hit. I knew he was drunk to the point I hated him, but I loved him too, because he was there.

I was reckless but smart. I was always ahead of my years. That was both a good and a bad thing. I made many mistakes, but my definition of making mistakes is that you can look back on them and correct them as your life unfolds. So, I really wouldn't call them mistakes. Where do I start? The things I did, and saw were crazy.

↔

We moved to Hazelwood in the early 90s, and we moved down below the tracks, affectionately called 'Down Below.' Back in those days, there were still a few racists, if you ask me. There were more whites than blacks down there, but I loved it. The smell 'Down Below' used to make me sick because of the thick ass smoke from the Steel Mills. I was delighted to learn that they closed the Steel Mills years later.

Anyway, so 'Down Below' was the shit to me. My mother, brother, sisters, and dad moved to this little alleyway named Ladora Way. One thing about that street, man, it smacked OMG! As kids, we had fun, and not to mention that many of my family members moved to the same street. We had our aunts, uncles, and cousins all right there! We were having a lot of fun damn near every day and night. But there was a downfall to living on Ladora Way. There were a lot of drug dealers. We saw it all; there was nothing we *didn't* see. You name it, we saw it, which was kind of a bad thing, but it happened.

Nevertheless, they respected all the kids on the street. I remember when we first moved out of Hazelwood. There was a gang of dudes. The same ones that posted up on Ladora. They tried my dad and jumped him, and shit... he wasn't with it. He showed them the meaning of welcoming himself into the "JUNGLE."

Shortly after we moved to the 'Jungle', my mom got pregnant with her sixth kid, and that was her last. Dom always wanted a brother, and his wish was my mom's command. My baby brother Tel came, and that was the completion of my mom's tribe. Tel was spoiled and never had to endure what Nish, Dom, and I had gone through, and I'm glad he and the twins didn't. Like I said, it wasn't a bad childhood, but we had our days. More good days than bad days, but it could have been a lot more Better Days, if that makes sense.

Growing up in that house, between the love and the chaos, I learned early on what strength meant. Watching my mom work her fingers to the bone every day to keep us fed and clothed gave me a deep respect for hard work and resilience. She was the backbone of our family, the glue that held us together even when things got rough.

My dad, with all his flaws and battles, showed me another side of strength— the kind that fights silently against pain you can't see. He was tough, strict, and sometimes harsh, but I knew he did it because he cared. His alcoholism was a heavy shadow that hung over us, but underneath that shadow was a man who tried to protect us the best way he knew how.

Living on Ladora Way was a world of contrasts. Sure, the drugs and violence were real and scary, but so was the sense of community. We had family everywhere, and despite the hard edges, there was laughter, joy, and safety in those relationships. The street might have been "the jungle."

Looking back, pain was woven into our lives like threads in a tapestry, sometimes thick and dark, sometimes faint and soft. But those threads also connected us, held us together, and shaped who I am today. The pain wasn't just about hardship; it was about growth, love, and survival. It was about learning to rise even when the world tried to keep me down.

I had lots of memories. When we moved to Hazelwood, we started school. We went to a school called Burgwin Elementary, and I was in the 2nd grade. My teacher's name was Ms. Kuhn. She was an older white lady, but she was very nice. I met a couple of friends in 2nd grade. As the school year progressed, I made more friends, and by the end, the whole class had become my friends.

I always stood out. In everything I did and no matter the school, I was friends with everyone; white, black, and even those with handicaps. Everybody looked the same to me, and I treated everybody the same. My first fight, which I will never forget, occurred in the 4th grade in Mrs. O'Brien's class. This certain individual was known for knocking people out, and boy was I scared, but I could remember it was time to go. So, Mrs. O'Brien called us by the rows to retrieve our belongings from the lockers in the hallway, and she gave me that look and kind of growled at me, LOL. Man, I was about to shit bricks, but I growled back.

We walked back into the classroom, and it went down. We both had long hair, but I was so scared that I pulled every bead out of hers. She pulled mine out, too, but I didn't care. I was tired of her growling at me and bullying me. The whole class was happy that I stood up for myself.

Growing up in the 'Jungle' was a blast. We did all the typical kid stuff, from hide-and-seek and catching lightning bugs to fighting our siblings and cousins. There were good and bad times. I could remember one night my mom was at work, and my dad was drunk as hell and he had me, Nish, and Dom in a room, and I just remember him yelling at us. We were all crying so bad that he took an extension cord and tried to kill himself in front of us. This fucking devastated us.

We never knew why he did that but seeing that really made me look at my dad in another way for a long time. As a kid, I was thinking to myself, *How can a man so strong want to kill himself?* It left me puzzled, and I never wanted to relive that day again. Our dad was our hero, and I'm sure that scared my two siblings and me at that time. But that didn't stop us from loving him unconditionally. We were kids and eventually stopped thinking about certain things that went on in our younger years.

We were just happy to have him and our mother. In my early school years, as I mentioned earlier, we attended Burgwin Elementary School, and even after that, my friends followed me to Gladstone Middle, which was even more fun.

I started "smelling myself"; not being arrogant or conceited but just realizing my beauty. I started looking at boys but never knew what a boyfriend was. My first crush was in 5th grade. We'd walk home together, do homework, and kiss a couple of times, but it was nothing major. That was until I caught him and Nish kissing behind a car. I was so crushed that he even named his cat Nina.

Middle school was cool until they split up Gladstone into different neighborhoods. The Hazelwood kids had to go to the Hill District, while the Homewood kids attended a school closer to their homes. Guess where I went? To the North Side. I hated that my mom had enrolled me in a magnet program, and I attended Allegheny Middle School. I hated it. I swear, man, everything about it. I got into fights there, and the thing that stuck out the most was in September, I could remember being in the cafeteria and everybody was going home. It was when all the people were killed on September 11, 2001.

The attacks were a series of terrorist attacks by an Islamic group. Four planes were flying above the U.S. Two of them were flown into the twin towers of the World Trade Center in New York, another crashed into the Pentagon in Virginia close to the nation's capital of Washington, D.C., and another into a field in Pennsylvania. I was terrified. Only two or three kids were left at school that day. They called my mom and she didn't answer. I thought staying in school was crazy. I didn't really know what was going on at the time until my Mom explained to me, and I watched the news.

All I was interested in was getting home. I didn't know that day was just sad for me because I felt alone in a new school with no friends. I missed my friends so much. Although I met some really great people throughout the 8th-grade school year, I just had to adapt.

At the end of my 8th grade year I got into a fight and missed my promotion exercises. Honestly, I didn't care. That year flew by, and I was just happy to get out there. So, it was the summer before I entered high school. You couldn't tell me a damn thing. I felt like I was on top of the world. I had hips, breasts, legs, butt, and a very nice smile, and not to mention chocolate.

I was feeling myself a little too much until one day my stomach started hurting. I mean, bad cramps! I went to the bathroom. It was my menstrual period. I'd heard a lot about it, but that day, I experienced it firsthand. I thought, *Why me, man?* But if you know me, I didn't let that period stop me. I love my mom! But if you know me, I didn't let that stop me. Nope, I still was fresh and it was the summer, so that meant lots of boys, friends, staying out until the streetlights came on down below the shit hands down. We had fun.

I experienced so much that summer, from getting beat down for sitting on a guy's lap to my weed breakdown. Yes, I remember the first time I smoked weed was with my sister and her friend. I didn't know what type of weed it was, but it didn't agree with me at all, so I started tripping. I mean, real-life tripping. My heart was racing, and my fingers were tingling. I wanted that feeling to go away, and all while I was going through my "WEED BREAKDOWN."

My sister was scared like, "Nina, stop playing, man! Mommy gonna whoop my ass! You play too much!"

LOL, but I wasn't playing. I couldn't handle the weed. It felt weird as hell, and to me, it felt like I was high forever! But yet and still, I didn't get enough because a couple of weeks later, I was smoking with my little brother and went through the same thing.

But this time, I called the ambulance, my brother was so mad like, "Homies, you're killing my vibe really, Nina?"

Man, weed was not my thing at all, so I never tried it again. Life in Hazelwood wasn't always easy, but it was real. The neighborhood had its flaws— smoke from the Steel Mills that made you cough, streets full of people trying to survive in their own ways. But for us kids, it was just home, and with all of our family there, every day felt like a big, chaotic family reunion.

We had fun, even if the world around us wasn't perfect. School was a mixed bag— sometimes a place of friendship and laughter, other times, a battleground. I learned early that standing up for yourself wasn't optional. When you're a kid from the 'Jungle', you have to carry a little toughness in your bones. But inside, I was still just a girl trying to find where I fit. New schools, new faces, feeling like an outsider more than once, it all shaped how I saw myself.

At home, the fights and silence between my parents taught me that love can be complicated and painful. Watching my dad struggle with his demons, and my mom holding it all together, left scars I carried without fully understanding them at first. That night, when my dad almost gave up on himself, it shook something inside me forever. But even then, I loved him— because sometimes love means holding on, even when it hurts.

And then there was that summer— the one where everything changed. The excitement of growing up, of feeling noticed, mixed with the chaos of those first mistakes and new experiences. Trying weed for the first time and feeling it hit harder than I expected was just one piece of that puzzle. I was learning who I was, what I could handle, and what I wanted to leave behind.

Looking back, those years were messy but real. They weren't perfect, but they were mine. And through every fight, every heartbreak, every wild night, I was building the foundation of the woman I'm still becoming.

In the summer days, like I said, there were boys, boys, and more boys. I had my eye on one, and while I had my eyes on him, he had already had his eyes on me. He was a chocolate, muscular guy who had just moved into Hazelwood. What's crazy is that our birthdays are just a couple of days apart, which is what drove me crazy about him. We used to just flirt and talk on the phone until we fell asleep.

Then, one summer day, it happened. I had friends who had already had sex, so I had heard stories of it, but I never had sex. I never thought I'd experience this part of life. For some reason, I always planned things out; however, this wasn't planned at all. But I knew that I liked this boy, and he was the one for sure.

What's so crazy is that in certain movies, I used to see people kissing and touching, so I had that in my head. I had known he was experienced just by the way he touched me that hot, sweaty night; even his kisses were mature! He went slow for the most part, but I was anxious. I didn't know about foreplay.

I was young, and I just wanted to experience the feeling. At that point, I was definitely curious. Once that moment happened, I knew it was real. It took some time to adjust to the feeling since I was a virgin. Still, it happened. I felt like a superwoman, but then I felt like *damn*. How am I going to tell my mom?

I hid the fact that I wasn't a virgin for a while. It just didn't seem real the rest of the summer. I thought about that day, but I don't know why I overplayed it in my head day in and day out. My friends would often share their experiences, and mine were always different.

He took his time, and it wasn't a rush at all; it was just me and him. He was a true gentleman and coached me through it! He taught me the basics...I lost my virginity the summer before going into the 9th grade. Who would have thought?

Even after that day forward, I knew that my life would change. Throughout my teenage years, I felt alone, not physically, but emotionally. I had love around me in the form of family and friends, and I'm big on family to this day. But I suffered from abandonment issues and didn't even realize it until I got older. Not having my biological father around really set the tone as to why I lashed out in several ways.

I dated dudes in hopes that I could find the love I always wanted from my father. But having the love from my dad, I didn't play about how I knew I was supposed to be treated. I even started hanging around guys just to get a male's perspective and I continue to do so, this very day. I have friends from over 25 years who believe opinions matter, and I sit and talk to them just so I can hear how men think.

Then there was high school. Fall hit, and it was time to go back to school. My mom had sent me to Brashear, the weakest school in Pittsburgh, but I met some okay people there. I just wanted 9th grade to be over, and it went by quickly! I really didn't do much in 9th grade, but I failed all my classes and dressed just to go to school. I was a cute dummy. As long as I was in the building, I felt like it was right, and boy, was I wrong.

Eventually, 9th grade came and went, and I convinced my mother to let me attend Allderdice High School for the remainder of my years, and she agreed. Aye, what can I say? I always wanted to be an Allderdice dragon while I was in Brashear. That's all I thought about because my sister and her friends were up there.

I remember skipping school in Brashear because my sister went to school at Allderdice and there was going to be a big fight. Let me back up. My sister was the aggressor. She didn't take any stuff. She didn't like anyone, and nobody liked her. Nobody!!! And yes, she was okay with that; she had made a name for herself, and she was not the one to be messed with. Her behavior didn't just start in high school.

My sister had been fighting all her life, and I was always right behind her, even though some of her enemies took a liking to me. I was never breaking that code. You don't like my sister, you don't like me, period! I have so many memories of us getting followed home from school because somebody wanted to fight us. It used to go down; we used to call ourselves 'DBGs' the 'Down Below Girls'. 'DBGs' were made up of me, Nish, and two of her friends.

But back to the fight up Allderdice, it was at the end of the year, and my sister was in mode with the East Hill girls. And it went down; that was the school I wanted to be in. I liked the excitement, and that's exactly what I got. Brashear was like a shack compared to this big mansion in my eyes. It was perfect, and not to mention, I was in school with my friends, the ones I grew up with and the ones who know me. I felt right at home. Allderdice was a world apart from Brashear.

The halls buzzed with energy, the lockers slammed with the noise of a hundred teenage dramas, and every day felt like a new challenge. I was no longer just a face in the crowd— I was part of something bigger, something louder, and something that demanded attention. The fight my sister was involved in wasn't just about schoolyard squabbles— it was about respect, territory, and standing your ground. I watched her with a mix of awe and fear. She was fierce, unyielding, and fearless.

That strength inspired me, but it also meant danger was never far behind. The friends I made at Allderdice were different, too. They knew my family, my story, and they didn't shy away from the rough edges. We shared more than classes— we shared secrets, fights, and dreams about what life could be beyond Hazelwood. But beneath the tough exteriors, we were all trying to find our way. Some of us wore armor, others carried wounds no one could see.

Even though I wanted to prove I belonged, there were days I felt invisible, lost in the noise, and unsure of who I was supposed to be. High school was as much about survival as it was about growth. Every hallway was a battleground, not just for respect, but for identity. I was learning quickly how to navigate the politics of friendship and rivalry, trying to keep my guard up while still holding onto the girl inside who wanted to be loved and understood.

And then there was the pressure of growing up fast. The innocence of childhood was slipping away, replaced by the weight of decisions I didn't always know how to make. I was chasing love and acceptance in ways that sometimes hurt more than they healed.

My relationships with boys became a mirror— I was searching for something steady, something real, but often found only confusion and pain. At home, things weren't getting any easier. The silence between my parents was thick with unspoken words, and the fights left marks that didn't always show on the skin. I carried that tension with me every day, a reminder that love doesn't always come easy or clean.

I wanted to protect my family, but sometimes, I felt like I was the one who needed protection. Still, through all the chaos, I held on to my dreams. I wanted more than Hazelwood's streets and Steel Mill smoke— I wanted a life that felt like my own. I didn't know exactly what that looked like yet, but I knew it was out there, waiting to be found.

Those years shaped me in ways I didn't fully understand at the time. They taught me resilience, the power of loyalty, and the painful beauty of growing up too fast. Looking back, I see now how every fight, every heartbreak, every wild summer night was a piece of the foundation I'm still building on today. Nothing but love! I felt safe, but being in high school is very important, and you go through a lot of things, especially me. I started to let my grades slip again because I didn't care that I was a loose cannon that year.

I had met another young man who really changed my life. I met him on Second Avenue while walking to the store with my friends. He kept beeping at us, to be beeped at was crazy to me. I was the shit, and I felt like I was too good for him to beep at me.. LOL. But when he pulled over at the next light, he greeted me very strongly, and it turned me on. He looked a lot older, but he was my age. This threw me off because he was driving and had a baby seat in the back.

We started talking. I could always use a friend; whether it was good or bad, I didn't care. I thought I could handle anything, seeing he was a different breed. Even though he was young, he was hungry for money, and that drove me crazy about him. As months passed, we became closer. So close that I finally knew that the car he was driving was his mom's and the car seat was his little brother's.

By then, I had told my mom that I was having sex, and although she wasn't a fan of it, I didn't care. I was cocky. I had made my own appointments to get birth control. I had always heard about babies and STDs, and I didn't want either one. I wasn't with it. I used to stay over at his mom's house, and what was so lovely about him was that his mom lived right around the corner from Allderdice. I was in heaven.

We used to play in a playhouse in his mom's apartment. I fell in love, but everything came crashing down when he asked me to come over one night.

I was like, "Okay, why not?"

Now, mind you, it was a cold, snowy night, so I called a cab, which took an hour to arrive. I finally got to his house. I was cold as hell. Banging on his mom's door, no answer. His mom finally pulled up. I greeted her, but I was so mad she could see it in my eyes. I started to tell her how her son had called me to come over, but he was not answering his phone.

The cab has left and he's not answering the door either. She had let me in; she always knew I was over her house. Hence, she had no problem with letting me follow her up the steps. As I walked up the steps to get to his room, he came out.

I was like, "Man, what the fuck? You got me outside in the cold."

I walked past his room and headed to the bathroom, where I found a girl sitting on his bed, looking scared to death. I was so crushed that all I could do was walk out of his damn house; I just couldn't understand why. I knew it wasn't going to last.

He had anger problems as well. He physically abused me at one point in time, all because I thought it was right so that I allowed it. I was in high school with a black eye. I was hard-headed. I remember going to his house to stay the night just like any other time. My school was right around the corner from his house, so I used to go there and then head to school in the morning.

Well, the next morning came, and we had gotten into a big fight. I tried my hardest to walk away, but I always wanted to get my point across, and so did he. I don't really remember what the fight was about. Still, I just remembered a big argument and my hands started moving. I was never the type to back down.

All of a sudden, BAMMMMM! He punched me in my face. I tried my hardest to fight back. Still, I couldn't. He was strong, even his grandmother, who was in the other room, couldn't stop him from attacking me. I just balled up and stopped fighting back. Eventually, he stopped.

All I could think about was being in school and having to go home with this shiner on my head. I didn't go to school that day, so I called a jitney. It seemed like they had driven to my mom's house in two seconds. I arrived at my mom's house and opened the door.

My mom was in the dining room. I looked at her. She started screaming and yelling, and all I could do was cry that my boyfriend was hitting me. I could remember her calling the police. They told me to press charges, but I was so in love. I didn't go through with it. I continued to date him, and the abuse continued for months at a young age. I had experienced abuse, and it was not okay to go through what I went through.

I loved him, and I always said I would walk away. It was so hard because that's what I always dreamed of, but I want to tell you ladies and guys, if you're getting abused, "LEAVE." It's not worth it!

This book is to inspire someone experiencing any type of abuse. I can't tell you what to do. Yes, I say leave, but you're your own person when you're ready, and it's time. My book is real, and nothing is fake about it. My abuse came to an end when he became incarcerated. I was free and was able to forgive him and forgive myself, even with being in high school. I experienced a lot of good and bad things that ultimately worked out for the better in my eyes.

It taught me at a young age not to move so fast, but being young, I was just looking for "love." When I was in the 11th grade. What can I say? I was almost done with school. I fought hard. I had let my grades fall, but to fall is to get back up, and that's just what I did. I attended night school, Saturday school, and summer school.

By the end of my junior year, I had completed my graduation project. I was proud of myself, especially for overcoming the struggles I faced in life, both with friends and in self-discovery. Even with all that I've been through, I still didn't learn. I was the true definition of being hard-headed.

Another highlight of my life was months after the turmoil of my last relationship. I knew it was the end of my troubles, but it was the beginning of more. It all started when I thought I had moved on from my last relationship. Now, I was sure that I was ready. I never really planned relationships and friendships out. It just happened. One day, my friends and I were walking to the Dairy Mart when we heard a car driving past us. The music was blasting as the car pulled up into the parking lot. My whole life changed. Yes, I had met another dude, and this one caught my eye only because of his glasses, LOL.

Believe it or not, I had never seen a nigga riding around Hazelwood that wore glasses blasting music.

My friends were like, "Nina! Hell to the no, let's go!"

But I couldn't resist. His conversation was also on point, and you could tell he was older than I. The discussion was fascinating, but I could tell my friends were getting a little impatient while we were talking, so I talked them into getting in the car with me because I wasn't going to leave my friends and get in the car with a nigga I didn't know at all. They agreed, and we went for a ride just vibing, talking, and laughing.

All I kept doing was looking at him, trying to figure out who he looked like. I finally got it! He looked like Arthur from the TV show on WQED, but he was very nice to me. But then again, I had dated a couple of nice guys in the last two years. These relationships didn't work, but I was still looking for 'THE ONE.'

One night, we all had fun...and the next few months, shit got real. The thing about me is that when I want something, it becomes mine. I was young, wild, cute, and just didn't care. But with this relationship, I was blinded by a lot of things. He had already had a son, a baby momma "PROBLEMS," but by then, I didn't care.

We were together every day of the week, and he met my family, I met his, and life was great. That was my boo, despite a

couple of odds and ends. I thought for sure he was the one until....
He got incarcerated, and everything started coming out even more
than when I first heard. Now, as I mentioned, he had a son and a
baby mom, but I never knew his age because I never asked. I didn't
care. He looked young to me, but, as I mentioned earlier, I could
tell he was older just by his conversation; that's all that mattered.
However, being in jail gives you a lot of information about a
person.

Come to find out, dude was 21 and I was 17. "WTF!" I
knew for sure when my mom found out about this one, she was
going to kill me. But like I said, I was head over heels for him and
was still talking to the guy from my previous relationship, but he
was in placement.

I was juggling two guys at one time and both were
incarcerated. One was in jail and the other was in placement. I was
totally distracted by life and schoolwork; it was tough for me to
graduate because I was 'boy crazy'. Finally, after four long years of
high school, I graduated from Taylor Allderdice High School.

Becoming an adult was a rush after high school. The next
year, I finally left my previous relationship behind and just wanted
to be loved by the one person I thought loved me. I waited for
D.O. to get out of jail. I was excited. After high school, I initially
intended to attend college but my struggles in high school led me
to put my college plans on hold. To be honest, I just wanted to
have fun.

I moved out of my mom's house and went to stay with one
of my best friends, and that was the party house. I remember that
year because I had gotten my tongue pierced. LOL! I just knew I
was grown. I was hustling, making money, going out drinking, and

staying out all night. I just didn't care; I was wild, and I couldn't help it.

Until one day... I will never forget. I wasn't feeling good, and I could also remember it being a cold ass winter day. I was down at my friend's house. I had no clue why I wasn't feeling right.

So, she's all like, "Bitch, let's go get a pregnancy test."

I looked at her like, bitch I'm not pregnant, even though I knew I was in a relationship with D.O. and having unprotected sex with him. Still, my mindset was, "I'm Nina, wasn't nothing stopping my show." I took the test and walked out of the bathroom five minutes later.

My friend walked into the bathroom, cracking up like, "Yeah, okay, YOU'RE PREGNANT."

I was shocked like hell. Not to mention, I had missed my birth control doctor's appointment. But I didn't even realize it as my life was moving so fast. I was confused and shocked. I eventually told D.O., and I just went on with the pregnancy.

Honestly, I had a pretty good pregnancy until he decided to go to jail again. I was so over the jail thing and didn't want my child to be subjected to that lifestyle. A couple of months before I had my unborn child, he came home. It was always a love-hate type of thing because he couldn't stay out of jail. I had always loved him.

I have known him for years. That was my heart. High school was a turbulent time, a complex mix of emotions and experiences that shaped me in ways I didn't fully understand back then. It was a place where I often felt like I was walking a tightrope, trying to balance between who I was and who I wanted to be, all while navigating friendships, relationships, and the pressure to fit in. Love, or what I thought was love, came wrapped in complications.

There were moments of warmth and connection, but also times when I endured hurt and betrayal. It was a confusing dance between holding on and knowing I should let go. At the same time, I was learning hard lessons about self-worth and boundaries, even if I didn't always act on them. The emotional bruises left marks that weren't visible but ran deep. School was both an escape and a battleground. My grades slipped as I wrestled with inner turmoil, but beneath it all, there was a fierce determination to rise above it.

I surrounded myself with people who understood the streets and the struggles, friends who were like family, offering some sense of belonging. Yet, the sense of loneliness never quite left me. I was learning who I was, figuring out what I could endure, and trying to protect my heart while still yearning for love and acceptance.

I want you to really know me— not just the surface stuff, but the parts that didn't make the highlight reel. I was proud and stubborn, sometimes to my own detriment. I carried a toughness on the outside, but inside, I was often scared and unsure. I made mistakes— some I regret— but each one taught me something valuable. I was learning to stand up for myself, even if it meant getting bruised in the process.

I wasn't perfect, far from it. I was a girl who just wanted to be loved and to feel like I mattered. I had dreams and hopes, even when it felt like the world was stacked against me. And despite everything, I kept going— sometimes because I had to, other times because I believed there was more waiting for me.

Looking back, those years were a blend of pain and growth, confusion and clarity. The challenges I faced taught me resilience and grit. They pushed me to become tougher, but also made me realize the importance of healing and self-love. It was the foundation of everything I am becoming— a woman still learning, still growing, and still striving for peace and happiness.

But things never really pan out the way I wanted and pictured them to be, just like this little baby coming. I knew he/she would give me trouble even before the arrival into this world for three reasons:

1. The day I went to find out the gender of our baby he/she wouldn't open their legs. (I came to find out weeks later it was a girl).
2. She was due October 13th and didn't arrive until October 25th, 2007.
3. The labor was unbearable. I thought I was about to die. I could still remember that I had to get induced.

↔

My mom had left because she was taking too long to come, and I was so scared. I had an excellent support system when it came to my unborn child, so while my mom was at home, my sister was there with me by my side every step of the way. The contractions hit me like a ton of bricks. My palms were sweaty. I just knew I was going to die on the bed giving birth to my baby.

I could hear my sister saying, "Nina Push."

I kept saying, "Nish, I can't!"

I was yelling at her, growling and crying, telling her I was in pain, and I couldn't do it.

Nevertheless, I couldn't push her out, so after I pushed for hours and hours, the doctors said, "We're just going to have to give you a C-section."

I was so scared, but of course, my sister was there, so we proceeded into the operating room. Seeing all those big lights and tools to start the procedure, I was shaking. Then I looked over to my right, and I saw the scale they put the baby on after delivery. I got excited. So here we go.

The procedure began with the doctor giving me a shot in my back to numb me. I didn't feel it at first, then I felt it. My legs felt like I was weighed down with a ton of bricks. I couldn't see anything, as they had a white cover-up during the procedure, but I knew I was okay. I had my sister by my side every step of the way. She made sure I was okay and watched Da'Najah Ann Owens arrive in this world firsthand.

I didn't feel the cut, but I felt her getting tugged out of me, and there we have it. An 8-pound 9-ounce baby girl entered the world. I heard her cry, and it made me cry, but I couldn't see her due to the white covering and because I was getting stitched and stapled.

All I could think about was kissing her and seeing what gift God gave to me. After weighing and cleaning her off, there she was, so beautiful. She was so chunky, and she had the same cheeks that I have. And a head full of hair despite going through so much pain having her and being two weeks overdue. I didn't care. I fell in love with everything about her.

I could remember her dad coming into the room after the delivery, trying to take pictures.

I was like, "Nigga…. Please, you weren't even there for your first daughter's birth."

But I didn't let that stop me from being the best mother I can be. I already had an apartment, and it was perfect for me and Da' Najah.

The best part about Da'Najah is that she showed me what's real. She showed me the true meaning of love, in her own cute way. I remember I had to put her in her baby bouncer and sit her in the bathroom, running water just to stop her from crying. She was a real live brat. Still, I had her like that; she was my firstborn.

Boy, oh boy, did Naj give me a run for my money? Even to this day, she remains powerful. I can say she gets that from me because I, too, am very dominant and very outspoken with my words. I often look at Naj and I get sad because she is me all over again, and it hurts me. Her father spent thirteen years in jail, and that affected her so terribly. I saw the same hurt that I felt inside on her face because her father went back to jail a couple of months after she was one year old.

I did everything for her, and I felt like I could never let her down. I worked hard for my baby. I was her hero. What I loved about Naj was that she quickly picked up on things I taught her, even after I showed her just one or two times, and she mastered them. I don't know, but I kind of raised her to be independent because I couldn't imagine my life with any other children at the time.

There was nothing she couldn't do. She held her bottle, early in age, and the amazement was at an all-time high. Even on days when I felt like I was less than a mother, she showed me I was perfect enough for her. Raising a very intelligent, smart, and challenging child can have its ups and downs, though, because it comes with a lot of questions. She questioned me about why her father wasn't around, and eventually, I told her the truth. But, as I mentioned earlier in my book, I didn't think my mom should have told me about my history, but I did it anyway. I always say that who you come from doesn't define you; it's who you become that matters.

So, I'm not sure who I'm speaking to, but listen, first-time mothers, you can do it!! The road may be hard at first, but the outcome will always get better. Never stop and don't give up. I will say this, though: give your child whatever help they need to get, whether it's mental or emotional.

I raised Naj off my emotions, and I didn't know any better, so I guard her with my life, even to this day. Naj was my little bestie. It was always just me and her. If you were around during Najah's baby and toddler years, you could understand why I always made sure she was taken care of to the best of my abilities. To be honest, that is where I went wrong. I know that it takes a village, a good village, a strong and consistent one to raise a child.

Don't try to do it all yourself because life itself is hard enough. So, if you have help, take it, and I do mean genuine help. My strength and ability were what helped me raise Naj on my own. You literally must be willing to fight no matter how many times you lose and get back up. You have someone who looks up to you and calls you mom. *Life After Better Days* will show you my life, whether it was good or bad. Also how to survive in this cold world, including how to shed light on your dark days. After getting adjusted to motherhood, life was okay. Najah's dad was in and out of jail, but I adjusted to just being with her and loving on my child.

Five months after Najah was born, I met a guy named SJ. SJ seemed to be quiet; all he did was stare at me. I could remember getting off the bus, and he'd be on the third-floor complex window looking down at me. I never was head over heels about anybody I ever dated at first, so I would always walk right past him.

Weeks went by, and he finally had the courage to speak. I honestly thought he was scared because of my demeanor and the way I just minded my business, especially living in a project (housing complex). That day, I wasn't quite ready for his approach, but I let him proceed with the couple of questions that he asked me.

After that meeting, we just hit it off. SJ was patient, and I started to like him. Nevertheless, I didn't really do my homework on SJ; he had a way with his words. He was a smooth talker. He didn't say a lot, but he said enough, if that makes sense. He was charming like the rest of them, but something caught my eye about SJ. One of my favorite cousins finally convinced me to talk to him so I gave SJ a chance.

What I loved the most about him was that he loved Naj. Secondly, what was so interesting about him was that we didn't have sex right away; we mainly talked and drank. He and his boys used to have rap sessions in my kitchen. I was just letting things roll and enjoying the fact that I thought I had my ideal man, but in the back of my mind, I knew that I had just had a baby five months ago, and that I really didn't know his motive.

After having a deep conversation with SJ, he finally told me that he had a 7-year-old son and a newborn daughter. I should have just picked and walked away right then and there. NOPE.... Wrong!!! I stayed. My five-month-old instantly bonded with him, which scared me at times. I also eventually met his son and newborn daughter, and we created a bond as well. It was all cool, and we became a couple, sex got put into play, and we started living together.

If you're following my story like I hope you would be, history really repeats itself. I met SJ with two children, and I had one. Does that sound familiar? It sounds like my mom and dad's situation, right? Life is crazy at times, huh? Life was going great, but one thing about living in the projects is that you typically don't know how people really are before you move into one of them.

As I became more comfortable, I started asking around, and to my surprise, I asked about SJ. I found out a lot, too. He was known for having his way with the ladies, and I wasn't surprised at all. I eventually felt like I was just next on the chopping block. While dating him, I met some amazing people in his family, though. One actually became my very good friend, more like a sister to me. We did just about everything together. At the time, she had two boys and a girl, and I had just had Naj, but I loved her.

She was so understanding and nonjudgmental. Those were the good days, when she taught me so much, and she probably doesn't even know it to this day. We used to make things happen for our babies. I'm forever grateful!

Back to SJ. We were boyfriend and girlfriend, and everyone knew we used to match our tennis shoes and go on dates. We both loved music. He even encouraged me to start driving later down the line in our relationship. I was in the clouds about this man, but eventually, things turned sour. We fell apart; we argued, fought, broke up, and got back together in a cycle of destruction.

In 2009, I had reached my lowest point in life, and it wasn't my fault, so it made matters much worse. Life threw everything at me all at once, but nothing could prepare me for the way becoming a mother would change me. Najah wasn't just my baby — she was my entire world wrapped up in a tiny, stubborn bundle. From the moment I heard her cry, I knew that no matter what pain or struggle lay ahead, I had someone depending on me, someone who needed me to be strong.

Even though her father wasn't fully present, I promised myself Najah would never feel alone. She was fierce and full of life, and I was determined to give her everything I didn't have. Motherhood pushed me to grow in ways I hadn't imagined. I learned to be patient when I wanted to scream, to fight when I felt like giving up, and to find joy in the smallest victories — a smile, a new word, and a hug. Najah taught me how to love unconditionally, even on the hardest days.

Meeting SJ was like a new chapter — a chance to build something bigger than myself. He wasn't perfect, and I wasn't ready to trust easily, but seeing how he cared for Najah opened a door I thought was closed. Together, we found moments of laughter and hope amid the chaos of the projects and the challenges that came with blending our lives. But love isn't always enough. The reality of our situation eventually caught up with us — broken promises, arguments, and the strain of trying to hold on when everything around us felt like it was falling apart.

Looking back, I realize those years taught me more about resilience than anything else. How to stand tall when the world tries to knock me down, and how to keep moving forward, no matter how heavy the weight on my shoulders.

This is the story of a young woman learning to be a mother, a lover, and most importantly, herself, through all the pain, all the mistakes, and all the hope that still burns inside. I found myself and my child homeless in 2009 with nothing.

Always pray and be grateful for what you have. Remain humble, because in a blink of an eye, it can be gone. (Note to Self) But one thing I did have was my sanity, God, and my mom. I had nobody to run to, and even SJ fell off. I felt cold and lonely.

But to know me, you should know that I can only be down for so long. After being homeless for a couple of months, I was fortunate to find another apartment. Trying to get back on my feet was a struggle, but I always felt like God put me on this earth to conquer a lot of things.

People say never question God, but for some reason, I wanted to at this time in my life. Being homeless made me angry. I loved my mother's house, but I didn't want to live there; I preferred to visit. I love living by myself; it gives me my own privacy. All I could think about was the situation that led me back to my mother's house. Da'Najah, SJ, and I were all I could think about. As I mentioned earlier, I was fortunate to have experienced that life lesson, which has shaped me into who I am today. I look at life differently now that I've paved the way in my spiritual journey, but during my storm, I became bitter for a long time. However, life goes on, and I had to forgive, but not forget.

Let me rewind back to thanking God for giving me hope and strength to receive another apartment. At this point, I didn't have an option on the location where my child and I, along with SJ, lived, but it was just a steppingstone. I hated the location; it just wasn't for me, but nevertheless, we had our own. After all that was going on in my life, I knew a blessing was coming my way.

One day, I felt so sick like I was going to die of a sweating fever. My body didn't feel right at all; SJ and I were lying in bed. I was balled up with the shakes, no bullshit, within the next ten minutes, I told SJ to call the paramedics. I was in the ambulance truck really feeling like I wasn't going to make it there. I was afraid.

We got to the hospital after a short drive. They ran over ten tests on me and there was nothing wrong. This really scared me. I was literally sick, and the doctors were looking at me like I was half crazy.

I felt terrible when the doctor came back into the room and said, "Ms. Porter, before we discharge you, can you do this last thing for us? Can you give us a urine sample?"

In about ten minutes, the same doctor came back in and told me, "Well, I know why you're feeling awful. You are pregnant."

Yes, again, but the difference was that this pregnancy was planned. I wouldn't say planned but was SJ and I talked about having a child one day. My first pregnancy wasn't planned, but it was accepted, and both were made in love. The only thing was, I never felt so horrible in my life.

I came home and told SJ, and he was like, "I knew it."

I was so excited, even when I found out that I was having another girl. I didn't care about all the things I was going through.

She was my blessing! After nine months and three days of being overdue, my second pride and joy arrived on November 18th, 2010. Sa'Marah LaNay Jackson, I was thrilled to give birth to Moot, which is what I affectionately call her. I had a tough pregnancy, but what's crazy is that Moot was the happiest baby ever. All she did was smile. She barely cried at all.

Even as a toddler, she hated to cry. I can remember her getting in trouble with me, and she held her tears in. She eventually started crying, but Moot was strong. She's very quiet and observant, but she hates conflict. I was happy that she was a good baby because Naj was a lot harder to raise.

Sa'Marah is my replica. She is my twin, and it felt so good. I had her dad by my side. It took me back to how I always wanted to have a family. SJ had already had a son and a daughter, so my family was complete. I loved his kids and he loved Da'Najah. Life couldn't be better. Things were finally in place, but of course, time reveals a lot of things. However, I was happy and that's all that mattered.

I was happy. At that moment, I had two daughters, but I knew SJ was always up to no good. I will never bash anyone and tell their story. All I can do is share my own experiences, and I will tell the truth about my life, especially if someone is involved in my story or journey. We had a lot to work on in our relationship.

SJ couldn't hold a job for long and didn't have a hustle to save his life. I always worked, though, and I held us down even when I stumbled between jobs; I made things work. I made some bad decisions and was trying to survive, I made things shake. There were times when I couldn't even get the jobs I wanted because of the decisions I made in my life.

Life got really tough for me, but I had to get it together. It didn't matter. Survival mode was the only thing I could think about. I was into scamming, forging checks, stealing out of stores, whatever it would take to care for my babies. I wasn't proud of the decisions I had to make, but to learn your lesson, you must make mistakes.

I was hungry for money. I had always seen my mother pushing to get up and get to it, and I followed in her footsteps. I had a job, and I felt like that still wasn't enough. I was just super raw at coming up with ways to get the bag.

I love my life. It taught me the ins and outs of being book smart as well as street smart. I promised to love my girls and to always take care of them by any means. From day one, I've always known that being a good mother meant doing whatever it took. My girls are my life, and if you know me well enough, you will understand that everything I do is centered around their well-being. Every decision I make is based on their needs and interests.

It started to get strange with me and SJ as Sa'Marah got a little older. I always wanted the white picket fence, the family, marriage, and the whole fairytale life. I dealt with things that I would NEVER deal with right now, and I AM NOT PERFECT, nor will I ever play victim, but damn. God makes no mistakes, and I stand by this. I always hear the saying, "Don't have a second baby by the same man that hurt you," blah, blah, blah, but yes, indeed I did. But my second child came years later. I'll get to that in my journey of purpose.

In 2009, I was in that space — somewhere between survival and surrender, praying for a breakthrough while trying to hold on to my sanity. It's wild how quickly life can shift. One moment you're maintaining, and the next, you're counting blessings just to have your mother's door open and a warm place to sleep. I wasn't out on the streets, but I didn't have a place to call my own — and that kind of displacement hits deep when you're a mother. It made me question everything, even God. I was exhausted and empty, so I would ask, "Why me?"

Still, I kept going. I had no choice. My daughters needed me, and deep down, I knew I wasn't built to stay down for long. I've always had this fire inside — this voice reminds me, you don't stay broken, you rebuild. When I finally got that new apartment, it wasn't in the best neighborhood. In fact, it was far from ideal. But it was ours. A roof, a space, a fresh start — and sometimes that's all you need to catch your breath.

But it wore me down. I started noticing things. The way I'd walk into a room and feel like I didn't even exist. The support only came when it was convenient. The way love started to feel more like survival than a partnership. I felt like I was begging to be seen while giving pieces of myself away that I'd never get back. I wasn't bitter — not yet — but I was exhausted.

The more I fought for us, the less fight I had for myself. And that's when I knew something had to shift. I didn't want my daughters growing up thinking love looked like settling. I didn't want them to mirror my sacrifices — I wanted them to inherit my strength. There's a very real grief that comes when the family you imagined starts to unravel in front of you. But I held on for as long as I could. For the sake of the girls. For the sake of what we'd built. For the sake of the dream.

And I also held on because I feared starting over. Again. But God has a way of stripping you bare just to rebuild you stronger. And that's exactly what He started doing. Quietly. Patiently. Faithfully. Even while I was still trying to keep everything from falling apart, He was already laying the foundation for my next chapter.

I knew that the relationship wouldn't last, but I took the risk. Love is an addiction. Even if you aren't in love, the memories of what you thought was love can tend to play mind games with you.

I remember finding out I was pregnant with Aa'Layah and feeling like I was starting over with all the pain and trauma I was going through with SJ. Still, I looked at it in a beautiful way; I was blessed, to say the least. There's a beautiful story behind her life that you'll read as you keep going on the journey of *Life After Better Days*. I never would say I made the same mistake twice because I didn't. After everything I've been through, everything we've taken each other through, I finally walked away after an 11-year on-and-off relationship.

FINALLY, when I left, I was broken, destroyed, humiliated, embarrassed, and disgusted, all because I didn't know my worth. I made the best and smartest decision. I was scared and confused with rage at how I would even go on with life because of how deep I let myself get. I knew that things would be different, and I was right. It was a cold world out there, and I had to bundle up. Friends turned into snakes, handshakes became fragile, and smiles started to sour as people picked a side, and I completely understood it.

Initially, I didn't because of how I saw certain people when my relationship with SJ was going on, but eventually, I got the picture: the whole part of me was forgiving. The saddest part about the whole thing was that I knew my children would suffer. I knew my days would be long and dark. Still, I never gave up as a parent. I'm speaking to male or female, if you see any early signs, let it go, it's not worth the heartache, the mental baggage, or the trauma.

I often wish I had a new me to guide my old me, but I wonder if I'd listen. PROBABLY NOT!!! Because I'm hard-headed. I was the type of person who would stick it out with you until I hated the situation or person, and that took forever. This can be damaging to you, the situation, and all the parties involved. Don't walk around playing happy just because you want the feeling; you must live it.

PAIN: Part II

The pain I endured, I just knew I could live through it because of how strong I became. I used it to my advantage. I came out swinging and kicking. Some also didn't think I could survive my life situations, but I did, even with bruises and trauma, I made it. I pressed through and did what needed to be done to try and survive the process, AND IT WASN'T EASY!

You can try to avoid and go around the pain, but you have to dig deep into your inner self. I had to stop complaining and use every ounce of energy to cope. That's what fueled my fire. I prayed so much, y'all. Just imagine if you could use your pain to fuel your fire and navigate through life. How cool would that be? More importantly, I want you to use your pain to heal, not hurt others. You have the power to forgive and start your healing journey.

I recently spoke with my second daughter's father, and he sent me a text thanking me for how far we had come. His youngest daughter's birthday party was truly a success, with him, my first daughter's father, and my significant other at the time being present. After reading over the text, I simply texted back, "I had to forgive you in order for our daughters to be happy." It isn't and never will be about us; we share two children together, so their happiness is what matters. I feel like all pain isn't negative. I used my pain to learn how to love more.

I got past the feelings part. I never paralyzed my pain. I sat in it. I found a mirror and took accountability. My perspective is that everything has made me better, not bitter. I came from a life full of pain, and I'll never let that make me scornful. I used the pain, NOT for revenge, but for my purpose. Talking to my inner self, I realized I wanted more. I wanted my daughters to be genuine. I had to ask myself, "What's the motive behind conditioning myself?" It was simply about living my true self and pouring into my daughters, all while trying not to damage them.

It hurt so much, it was so painful, but after I suffered, I knew that the reward was so much bigger because I still have so much life left. Closing the gap between pain and promising myself I would do better was always on my agenda. I almost let it define who I was as a young girl, a teenager, and currently in my adult life.

Pain is real, but it's temporary. Taking the necessary steps to not give up and stay focused is key. You'll cry and crumble, but if you persevere, you'll discover the positive side of it. My greatest asset was wanting to just heal. Some people refuse to heal. They might want to be damaged, or maybe they just didn't know how to fight through it, just like I did at one point. It's like, what do you do if and when a battle chooses you? What do you do when it shows up at your doorstep? Shit.... When you were born in it?

It's hard; the devil wants you to sleep with one eye open. But trust me, it's worth the fight. Just because you're afraid doesn't mean you have to live in fear. Let that pain go. The process is terribly hard when you have to keep reliving and visualizing the recurring trauma! Push yourself because you need to be healthy mentally. If you're willing to go through the pain, the pressure you put on yourself will promise that the past won't hinder your purpose. You will be the star player of this thing called life.

Don't be embarrassed by your situation. Half of the people are covering up the same pain with filters and smiles. Erase that way of thinking and take that mask off. Stay focused, you'll make it, I promise. Let it run its course. And remember, your life is not a race. Stay patient and keep going. Keep in mind that if you put the footwork in with the process of burying your pain, you are closer than you think to healing.

Some people have a lot to say about lives they've never lived, offering opinions on struggles they've never faced, and passing judgment on paths they've never walked. Trust me, I know the feeling, and I've learned to block it all out because nobody is perfect. Many of us got our backs against the ropes but kept fighting through the pain to stand tall. I was broken, and I still am. I have some broken pieces that I need to find the right ones to complete my puzzle. I speak of victory over my life.

I don't care what's going on; I speak positively every day, even if my day isn't going the way I wanted it to go. I keep going because I can only speak for myself if I sit in pain for too long. I become what my feelings are at the present moment.

The first thing I had to do was love myself. Life is too short. If you're still living, you have a chance! Now I'm not saying it will happen overnight, what I'm saying is don't give up. Pain.... Man, listen, I can go on and on, but *Life After Better Days* is a book to show you my life struggles, my highs and lows, but more importantly, to show you the outcome and what I did or I'm trying to do to overcome any situations I faced. Pain can lead to a negative mindset. The power over your pain is much greater than anything!

Being strong through pain is a testament to dedication and self-discipline, marking the beginning of your journey beyond the fear of the unknown. In my life, I didn't know... why from birth, but I had to put so much pain and childhood trauma behind me. It took 35 years, though. I lashed out in so many ways. Life is very difficult, but if you get rid of the doubt, pain, and fear, you'll be just fine. No one has it all figured out, but I also believe in knowing better so you can do better!!

What I've also learned in *Life After Better Days* is to sit in your pain, take a couple of deep breaths, and even if you can't control the situation at that moment, cry, get some alone time, meditate, and pray your way out of any storm. You have to forgive yourself and then lean in on forgiving others, accepting the pain, and not holding on, but knowing that it's going to get you to the next level in life. Feeling hostage isn't the way to go.

Pain is beauty and beauty is pain. You got this! Rebuild yourself... live your life like tomorrow is yours; hit the reset button and start living again. Some people were looking for help but not helping themselves. I had to rebuild my life. I told weakness to shut up. I gave excuses to be quiet. I had to get out of the abyss of misery. Cutting certain people off can be painful too; nobody talks about that, but it's needed. You need to have the strength to love yourself more. It's your life, and your strength is within you. Your flesh may be weak, but change is possible. Stop wasting time on negativity and look forward to *Better Days*.

People are hurting. I can say that I hurt, but we are human, and we have to find a way not to hurt people when we feel hurt. Everything you're reading, I've gone through. Trust me, I'm a walking testimony.

You have to have some integrity, morals, and values to endure pain. Trust me, those who had it *easy* wouldn't be the ones I'd look to for strength. They don't know my pain! They don't know what it takes to be tough! They don't understand the significance of rebuilding your life!

After years of pain, I can finally say that I'm healing. I'm human. I'M NOT HEALED YET, but I'm working on my inner self, and that outweighs life lessons. Trust the process, and even in *Life After Better Days*, I'll walk in my divine purpose to live happily, go through the trials and tribulations, my difficulties, hardships, and challenges, knowing that I'll overcome them because now is the time to navigate and find peace and prosper.

Trust me when I say, "You Got This." I often do groups at my current job with the clients.

I often ask them, "What are you going to do, lie down and die, or will you fight?"

Life itself is very hard, but when in doubt, you have God by your side. Nothing negative matters. I'm telling you all this to say, never give up!!! I used to sit back and overthink why my life was such a mess. I felt like my whole world was at a standstill, and I figured out that I had to start removing toxic people, things, and situations out of my life. What else I had to do was stop praying to

God for things that He knew weren't good for me. Until this very day, He is working on every move in my life. I ask Him daily to shield me because some days are easier than others, and it is hard to deal with some days.

It's all about how much faith you have in God and in yourself. Some people love to see you down, but not all of them. They thrive on other people's troubles; those are the ones you really need to watch out for. Believe it or not, it can be the closest person in your life, which is why you need to ask God to remove them.

Mental well-being is a very big one for me because a lot of people are not mentally stable. Now, let me say this: being mentally unbalanced can mess up every minute of your life, every second, if you're not happy or have a mental breakdown. I had a couple of them. Like I said earlier, my book will help you.

At a point in my life, I felt like WHY? Sometimes your mind can play tricks on you. It can make you think you need something or believe something, even when it's not true. It can put you in a state of mind where you think you're going crazy.

Listen, your sanity is everything. NEVER... I mean, never lose it, and if you do, please get it under control before it controls you. Coming back from losing your sanity is like being a baby all over again. You have to crawl before you can even start to regain strength, and sometimes, in many cases, your sanity is taken away by another person's actions and them hurting you. Life can really get you down; it will chew you up and spit you out, but the question is, can you overcome life? Life is a mystery.

You can be happy one day but then feel like your whole world is going to end. However, life is also what you make it. I've come to realize that for me to be genuinely happy, it starts with thinking positively. I think positively even when my yday doesn't start out like I want.

You can't let life always get to you, or you'll constantly worry that something bad is going to happen every time you wake up. I say live a little, get comfortable with yourself. It's all a part of mental healing. Another one that I want to talk about is physically being okay. Some of us can hide pain, but that's not good... (note to self). Some people look good on the outside but are really dying inside.

I meditated and prayed day in and day out. My life was intense. After many days, weeks, months, and even years of looking back on my life and the trials and errors I was born into and made myself, I've come to realize that I was finally starting to become happy and more grateful for the things that made me stronger, even if they caused me pain and trauma.

I published my first book, *Better Days*, and started to feel alive. I felt like my dark tunnel was finally coming to an end. My biggest challenge in achieving success as an author/publisher was forgiveness. That's why I always remind people that I motivate and inspire them to understand that even in their glory, they're still not perfect. The key is to work on becoming the best version of oneself.

Now, yes, I'm big on forgiveness, but it takes me a long time to do so. With that being said, while you're still trying to wrap your mind around what that person did to you, guess what? They are still living their life. You should do the same, even if you don't get any closure, forgive yourself and keep living. That's why I try to be true to everyone. I'm not perfect, but I want you all to know that everything comes from a genuine place with me. Forgiveness is huge!!

Before you forgive, learn to forgive yourself. After finally taking that step, my book sales skyrocketed. I hustled and grinded it out for my daughters, so they wouldn't ever feel the sting of rejection. I was, and still am, unstoppable. *Better Days* has reached over ten states that come to mind right now, and it's being embraced by countless people, both familiar and unfamiliar.

I feel so accomplished. The main thing I wanted to do was show my daughters that it can be done with hard work and dedication. If you don't know, my children are my life. My foundation is what always mattered to me. I speak life to them, granted life does happen. It always has, but as a learning mother, I'm learning to let them fall and be there to pick them up, but parents LET THEM FALL... Let your children make mistakes and let them know the consequences, even if they have to experience the consequences. If you keep trying to pick them up before they even fall, you will regret it.

My mom and I had a very deep conversation about this particular topic and she said the following to me, (Mind you, all of us are grown).

"I wish I had let you fall and learn at an early age."

Now, what she meant was that she never let us fall when we were younger. She was always there to pick us up and wipe us off. She wouldn't even let us get dirty. LOL. Fast forward to when we were teens, and I saw her enforcing things and letting us fall face first into any decision we made; we had to learn.

I soak in everything my mother says, knowing I look up to her. She's the real deal. She holds no punches; her beauty makes her even more beautiful. She's so put together and very inspirational. Even when I'm sad and frustrated, she always knows what a person is going through. I'm forever thankful. That is true, and I can honestly say that I've been through so much. I mean, being in a dark cave with no lights on, having to crawl my way out of a dark place, and still being able to get up and live. You have to fight for how you want to feel; the world can see the pain in your eyes, your posture, and your image.

Signs of depression and being stressed out can mess you up physically as well. Being in the wrong state of mind, overthinking, and feeling overwhelmed can lead to physical and mental exhaustion, causing your body and brain to shut down.

What else I found out about life is that some parts of your body don't have to function for you to survive, and this is just my opinion. Many people say, "Think with your brain," but do we really? After working in mental health, I work in a drug and alcohol facility. I often do groups with the majority of the women clients that's in recovery with an addiction. Still, as I sit with them and listen to their story and try to help them out, I have come to realize I'm addicted as well.

My uncle once told me, "Whenever you do your groups, show empathy, not sympathy."

I now understand what he meant. Even with myself, I always give my story empathy because I don't want sympathy; for what? Who benefits? Not me or anyone going through an addiction. I have a love addiction. Let me explain from start to finish. From the moment I was born, I entered this world without knowing how my life would unfold. None of us does. Because our lives were written out from the wound, I had my mother's and father's love, but not my biological father's. As a result, I learned to love people the way I wanted to be loved, and I just kept following myself. I'm BIG on love y'all, even with close friends, family, and my daughters. I'm filled with too much of it.

I always feel like I have so much to give (meaning love), but here is where my addiction comes in. Even when I don't have love to give, I try to find it. My cup will be bone dry, but I'll find a way to brighten someone's day or situation. I'm a LOVER! I overthink love and get overwhelmed because I hate seeing people or myself down or feeling unloved. Sometimes people play on a person like me.

One thing I will say that is also a downfall about having a love addiction is that when you encounter a situation or person that plays with your addiction, you tend to just go mute and eventually stop talking, you'll shut down because you can't even stomach the fact that any person can be so heartless, especially when they know your true intentions. I had to break that addiction fast. I know now, and I will never empty my cup for anyone for so many reasons. First, if your cup is empty, how can you even feel like you can help another out if you can't even help yourself?

Secondly, I also live by this. I can only give you what's overflowing out of my cup because it's falling out. That's extra, and I'm not stingy in any way, shape, or form. But what is in your cup is for you. Some may try to manipulate you into thinking your way of thinking is wrong, but it's not. Taking a step back from loving a person or trying to help the situation is your best bet. Also know that if your flesh is weak, you'll fall back into the love addiction phase, and that's when the cycle repeats itself.

Your mind starts to race, and then comes the problem-solving, extending advice, and attaching yourself to different people trying to help. Admitting this was my biggest step because I am working on this very thing to this day, even with me being a mother, my love addiction for my children is at an all-time high. I hate it when they have to go through things that have nothing to do with them. It was out of the selfish ways of humans, and each time I came to the rescue.

I overprotect just so my babies won't feel any pain. Now, I realize that I needed to ease up on hiding what they need to see. As my girls got older, I got a lot better at letting them have their own minds and opinions. I give them the floor to open up about any situation. I never shut my eyes on them and go blind, letting them lead the way. That's just not going to happen. But you must let them see the world with a clear-eyed view.

I slowly and do mean slowly detach myself from certain situations, so they'll figure it out. All in all, I never want my girls to feel like they don't have enough love, because again, having that love addiction kicks back in and goes into full effect. I love poetry, and you may also know, and I wrote a poem for Naj, Mar, and Lay, and it's called:

A Mother's Love:

Even in the wound, I knew how attached I would be,

Every movement, the gentle kicks and the stretching of my stomach made me happy.

Years later, I still feel the same, and no matter where life takes you,

Mommy will be in a car, plane, boat, or train, ready to wipe every tear away.

When the world is knocking you down, I'll be there. I will teach each one of you what life is about.

I'll instill so much knowledge and positive things into your mind, body, and soul that no one can take from you.

My love is stern; there's no time to hold your head low because the world sits high, and that's how I raised you, beautiful girls, to sit up high and walk with confidence.

A mother knows I do, and my mother did too.

To the world, I may just be a regular human, but to you three, I'm a superhero.

Every day, I tell you all I love you because I truly do, unconditionally. It's real and seen.

I will forever hold on tight, even when you're old enough to be Queens.

Love, **Mommy**

↔

With having three daughters, I went into savage mode. I was unstoppable for several reasons. I felt like I owed them so much after all we went through, from me and SJ. I prayed my way out of every emotion I was feeling. I started to become the woman I always dreamed of being in 2020.

I finally accepted the truth of my life, and when I did, I honestly didn't care about who was in my life or not. I WAS FINALLY IN ACCEPTANCE. Trust me when I say this; please, do not stay in any situation longer than you have to just because you have history with someone. That's the worst way to think.

I wish I could scream it out to someone right now because the comeback can take forever to get back to yourself. JUST

LEAVE the job, friendship, relationship, or whatever is robbing you of your sanity. Anything triggering your past and suffocating your future has to go. After a long battle of me wanting to be the bigger person and trying to make my children happy with being disrespected by their fathers, I just eventually went mute and stayed mute.

I will not be subjected to what I endured while I was weak, and there were times when I fell into the trap and got defensive, wanting my voice to be heard. I now understand that parents do not have to fight or even have any problems with parenting. It hurts the child. Even with one parent not being on board, it hurts the child; EVERYTHING HURTS THE CHILD.

Parenting has no handbook, and I just go with the day, down to the minutes and seconds. Each child is different. But what I won't do is ever give up on what I birthed, and that's NEVER, there is NO EXCUSE as to why a parent doesn't want to coparent. There are other sources of information on how to see your child, even if it's not in your favor. You don't even have to go through the other parent to be active in your child's life. That's a cop out. My girls suffered from this, and as a mother, I just made the best decision for them. How is it fair to see your child or children only on holidays? When you're alive, not in jail, and available? We all have our own opinions on this topic, and I'm not taking anything away from anyone's, but again, it's my life and story, and I'm telling it.

I will not raise my daughters in life to believe that a man or woman is supposed to keep walking in and out of their lives. I don't care if it was me. It's not fair... PERIOD!!! So yes, I am a mother who will raise her kids on faith and the best way I know how. Does it get easy? HELL NO!!! But will I give up? Hell, no! That's a NEVER.

My daughters make me who I am today. Each and every one of them has a special place in my heart. Let me just say this too, I AM NOT A PERFECT MOTHER by far, but I am a trying mother, and trust me, whatever we go through, my babies and I grow through.

Message to absent parents: Your children feel that void; they feel that pain. Some days are better than others, but all in all, they need you, not the toxic you or the one who wants to play the blame game, belittling the other parent, or even staying absent for your own personal reasons. I will say this as well: If you're not going to be consistent with parenting, stay gone.

Don't traumatize your child when you know you're not even willing to try. Some may not like what I wrote, but oh well. Do better! Our children owe us nothing. We brought them into this world, so figure it out or keep it moving. This isn't me dissing anyone or speaking out of anger. I really hope that if you are going through this, you can try to co-parent first.

If the other parent doesn't follow through, it won't work unless the parent is willing to try and stay consistent. *Life After Better Days* is about real-life situations that not only affect me but may also impact your life or someone you know. It's about rekindling a relationship with your child or being a single parent; ultimately, doing what's best for your children is the best approach. Live for you and your babies.

Who gives a damn what some people have to say? Because nine times out of ten they went through it, the scenario may just be a little different.

Keep praying! Keep moving! Keep going!

After following God's order, my children's fathers stepped up. None of us are perfect but we try! It's a battle within itself to raise children. All I ask for their fathers to do is try. This is my reality. There is no turning back who I brought a life into this world with, but I do believe in happiness, I believe in having a village. Keep up the good work to all of the fathers that are trying because Better Days are ahead.

PAST

PAST: Part I

How is it that we are able to walk away from the past? Well, you are aware of your pain, right? You chose to be no longer subjected to your past, so you learn to forgive and let go. You got to let go and release, and the only thing you can do is forgive. Acknowledge what happened to you and free yourself.

Purge it from your heart, New Beginnings, the present is a gift, and the future is waiting. Since I was a little girl, I felt broken dealing with self-identity, just knowing who I was. Where I came from, I resented many people, but the power of strength helped me let it all go. Choose to be free and put an end to your past.

I'm teaching my daughter this to this day. If you have children, talk to them. They go through life, too, especially if their parents are dealing with their past; it can bleed onto the babies. Ask them daily how they feel. I can honestly say that I was mad, bitter, and in shambles with how my life was written. I failed friendships, relationships, and how I lived my life, and I made mistakes. However, I've learned to let it go so that my daughters won't feel my pain any longer. I had to forgive their fathers for so much, in order for my daughters to be genuinely happy.

There's a saying: "Just because you spend a long time making a mistake doesn't mean you have to continue." I've learned that I had to go through my pain to bury my past. I've grown, evolved, and changed. I essentially realized that I am not a slave to my past. Ever since I was a little girl, a teenager, and an adult, I was scared to face pain. Now, I don't want you to think I had a horrible life because it was beautiful. I had a great childhood because I was surrounded by real love, but my adult years took a different turn, and I made mistakes. That's why I'm able to share my story; my life is my greatest gift.

I removed the mask of pain. I stopped running in place and just started running forward to my purpose! I found it interesting that I still see patterns, even though I've fallen into the way I thought life was supposed to be, not living according to my own story. I've also come to realize the importance of being grateful for the good days, the bad days, and the discomfort that lies ahead.

I go by the principle that in life, I always remind myself to choose happiness, even in my down season. I lived in a dark, lonely world, but I still had my head held high. I prayed for power even when I was powerless. It was painful, powerful, and required a lot of prayer so that I could be at peace.

You have to build your habits, and how they define you is how you will survive everyday life. It's like cultivating a delicate flower one day at a time. You also have to separate the old stories and be grateful for your new story. Meaning little action over time creates bigger results. We as humans must realize that we need to turn the page and that we are not yesterday's news or loss.

We have to calculate our ability to become something greater. The question is, do you believe it? You can create a new person. My message to anyone who is in their past stage in life: Do it for you!! Self-love is everything. Yes, change comes from breaking habits you want to break, but creating that mental space to heal is the best feeling ever. I'm so proud of myself, even when I feel like I've taken a step back.

After realizing I'm walking backwards into my pain stage, I sit in it, and then I flourish out of it and finish where I left off. I always ask myself, "Who will I choose to be?" I drop the ball at times, but I pick it back up.

Change is often met with resistance, but when we sense that change is in the making, our strength grows stronger. Your past does not define you. My past is so beautiful. It's an awkward picture from an imperfect human. I'm a legend, a champion, queen, mother, sister, daughter, aunt, publisher, author, and much more. I am somebody; I AM POWERFUL.

I speak life instead of defeat. I told myself the same story for years, but it didn't get me far. I had to rewrite my story and make improvements. Replaying your past will drive you insane. Learn and grow from every experience. Reprogram yourself. Your mind may be comfortable with the scripted story you are holding onto, and that can carry a lot of negative narratives.

Imagine looking in the mirror and saying, "I sat in my pain to overcome my past." In that moment, you'll see a glow; people will look at you and see a difference. Once you change the way you talk to yourself, the win will feel so accomplished. Put your past behind you, and you can find the willpower to look into your purpose. Bury it and try not to let it define you.

Sometimes the weight of the past feels heavier than the body that's trying to carry it. But over time, you begin to understand something sacred: you are not what happened to you. You are who you choose to become in the aftermath. And becoming requires release.

Forgiveness wasn't something I came to overnight, it was something I had to practice, every day, like prayer or breathing. I used to wonder why the pain lingered so deeply, even after people were gone or life had moved on. What I learned was that pain doesn't disappear just because you're in a new chapter. You have to close the old one consciously. You have to mourn who you were and forgive yourself for not knowing better at the time. I used to walk around angry at everybody. Angry at myself. Angry at love. Angry at how easy it was for other people to seem happy.

But eventually, I chose me. Not the broken me. Not the survival-only me. I chose the woman who was finally ready to heal— publicly, quietly, even when no one clapped for it. I say all of this because healing isn't a straight line. I didn't wake up and magically forget the nights I cried in silence. I didn't forget the abandonment, the betrayals, or the mistakes I made just trying to survive. I felt it all. But I also felt God slowly rebuilding me and whispering to me that I was worthy of peace.

I've made peace with the past. But more importantly, I've made peace with the version of myself that once lived in it and the version of me that didn't know how to protect her energy. The version that she thought had to prove her worth through people who couldn't see her. That girl deserves love, too. And now, as I raise daughters of my own, I teach them what I had to learn the hard way: that softness is strength. Asking for help isn't a sign of weakness. And you're allowed to start over, even from the middle of your pain.

The past doesn't scare me anymore. I revisit it only to remind myself of how far I've come. I don't live there. I no longer carry its burdens into my next chapter. And for those who do? I pray you find your freedom. Freedom is possible. Healing is real. And your story isn't over yet— it's just getting powerful. I think sometimes we forget that healing takes courage. Not the kind that looks loud or strong, but the quiet kind. The kind where you show up to your life, even when you're exhausted. Even when you're afraid that healing might cost you everything that's familiar. That kind of courage is the kind that changes you.

There were days I wanted to give up— not because I didn't want to be better, but because I didn't know how to be. I was still clinging to old patterns, repeating thoughts that told me I wasn't good enough, that I was too broken to ever be whole. But then I'd look at my daughters. I'd see their joy and innocence, and it would remind me: I don't have the luxury of quitting. I owe it to them to be the woman I needed when I was younger.

Letting go of my past was one of the most spiritual things I've ever done. I had to walk into rooms of my soul I hadn't visited in years. I had to feel pain I had buried so deep I forgot it even existed. But I also had to tell myself, "You survived this once. And now, you're going to survive it again— but this time, you'll heal through it." That's the difference.

I no longer wanted to merely get through life. I wanted to thrive in it. I wanted to smile for real, not for pictures. I wanted to wake up and not dread the day. I wanted to look in the mirror and see someone I respected, not someone trying to disappear behind makeup and a fake smile. And piece by piece, I became her.

It didn't happen all at once. It happened in the quiet moments. The nights I cried but didn't text anybody. The mornings, I still got up, made breakfast, and went on with my life even when my heart was shattered. The deep prayers... That's where the healing happened. Right there. In the middle of my real life.

I don't look at my past as a burden anymore— I look at it as proof. Proof that I didn't fold. Proof that I didn't give up. Proof that God kept me when I didn't know how to keep myself. To anyone reading this who feels stuck in their past: just know, there's no timeline to your healing. No deadline for your growth. You're not late, and you're not behind. Your story is still unfolding. Just don't be afraid to turn the page. There is so much beauty on the other side of survival. You just have to believe you're worth finding it.

PAST: Part II

I've always been the type of person who needed to experience pain to know it was real. It's a bit of a stretch to explain, but I know all my readers fell off a bike while learning how to ride it. I'm only asking because when you fell, you scraped your knee or even bruised your elbow, and you felt the pain.... And you got back up and kept trying.

That was me, but eventually, you get the steady flow of riding your bike, and you never look back at how many times you fell; yet, you never forget. That sums up my life. Once I get the hang of something, I go with the flow of life. I was, and still am, coming to terms with the fact that I am a hard-headed person at times. I will go through the fire with someone, whether it's a job, a friendship, or a relationship, and it takes me forever to walk away. But once I do, I let it burn, and that can be damaging to you and all parties involved. Don't walk around playing happy for anyone. Happiness should come from within yourself. Back to my life lessons:

Even through ups and downs, I'm raising beautiful queens, nothing less. I talk to my girls, and I give it to them real, never fake.

They will not grow up to be victims of anything, blinded and scared by the world. There are things that you are supposed to hide from your children, and I do, but there are also things that they should be taught in full effect; I teach them. They will not be weak. Yes, everybody has their weak moments, but I'm teaching them that even when nobody is there, they still have one another. I tell them that I won't always be here, but they should carry my name on and take care of each other.

To know me, you should already know that I let them know it's a cold world, so go into that jungle, kill that lion, and make yourself a fur coat. That's always been my motive. I can't even see myself raising anybody weak because I'm solid and strong. I get that from my momma. But I'm human just like everybody else. My struggles are real. I always talk to God and ask him for strength and the ability.

Also, I want to let my readers know that you're not alone; it's okay to cry, scream, or express your emotions. I've learned to always remain humble and to share my story to help others with theirs, and to never be judgmental because you never know what someone else is going through. Life can knock you down in many ways, leaving you without the financial means to survive, emotionally unprepared to handle daily life, mentally unstable, and physically unable to cope with the harsh world.

Believe it or not, I dealt with all of those at one time. Life hit me like a ton of bricks! I face a financial hit around the same time every year. Here are the things I always do to keep me balanced:

- First, without God's guidance, you have no way of figuring life out.

- Next, I prioritize my bills from most important to least. Some things are just wants, not needs, so I stock up on toiletries and food to prepare for the storm.

Remember, the storm doesn't last forever. Emotionally, you will be drained by life and what it has thrown at you. With me, I had so much going on, from relationship problems to when I was unable to breathe and understand love. I started loving myself more. Now, don't read too much into me loving myself; I've always loved myself. I have a very big ego! But everybody always has those days when they feel low and when they feel like, damn, I need to love myself a little bit more so I can remain humble to keep my sanity. If you didn't, that's okay.

My book may not resonate with everyone, but if it does, my words will help you. If you ever go through something similar, you can look back at my book and take notes.

Being emotionally tired is the worst because it starts to wear and tear on you, but after a while, I learned to Pray, Forgive, and Let Go. I also learned in life that things happen and that it's best not to question them. Don't question death, relationship problems, life, or troubles because you will drive yourself crazy. Ask me how I know? I had so many deaths around me that I couldn't grasp.

People who mean the most to me have passed away and left me broken. I speak on death because it can be a very emotional situation. I questioned each death. Honestly, death is very hard. It doesn't matter how long they have been deceased; if it was someone I shared my life with, I will mourn them. Even to this day, I hurt in silence about death. I often think about what life would be like if they were still here. Or dang, what are they doing right now?

I'm in my head about death because I often wonder if they went to heaven or hell. Yes, I think that deep, like, are they really resting? In peace that is... like how do we really know? How? We cry when death occurs, but why? Because our loved ones die? Yes, the flesh dies, but your memories hold so much more value. Right?

These are just the things I really think about, but because you don't want to, I think about how selfish we, as living humans, can be when our loved ones are suffering. However, I had to take a look at life and what I truly see in this thing called life. It's a beautiful feeling to have all of our loved ones around and living, but we all know that two things are for certain: we live to die.

If you know anything about me, it takes me a while to stop grieving but in some cases, why would you want your family members to suffer more than they currently are? I'm not saying that I'm not an emotional person, I am very emotional and a crybaby but I look at it as after death - comes life, and it hurts so bad. So, when I say that after death there is life coming, I strongly believe it.

My aunt Lonnie's death hurt me to the core. Now, looking back on the year she passed away, I didn't want to see her go. Many of my readers are familiar with my aunt Lonnie, as I dedicated my first book, *Better Days*, to her, because she will never be forgotten. Earlier in my book, I shared my story about my third daughter, who was a blessing to me. In 2016, when I was pregnant with Aa'Layah, my aunt knew I was expecting a child. I used to go to every hospital she was in just to let her know I was there for her.

After observing my aunt's lifeless body toward the end of her battle, I knew she was dying. She was tired, but she was a warrior. The crazy thing about my aunt's death is that my gender reveal was the day after her death. I remember this day like it was yesterday because we were all grieving her death and still trying to stay strong at my gender reveal, and to my surprise, I was having my third daughter. So, I was pregnant at my aunt's funeral. I was numb. I just couldn't believe she left us. I even lost faith in who I believed in because of her death. I just questioned, why?

Like, why would God take her? Why couldn't He just heal her body? Heal her so she could be back with her children, siblings, nieces, nephews, and her loved ones. She loved her family, especially her children. But as I thought about it after some years, I had to put my feelings aside and understand that my Aunt Lonnie's body was tired. She was in pain, and how dare I be that selfish when she was suffering mentally, physically, and emotionally?

She knew that Aa'Layah was coming into the family, so that was a new addition, and guess what? Lay was born on February 2nd, 2017, and my aunt's birthday is February 28th. So, I say thank you to my creator for having me understand death. I shared my life with you. I will mourn you. Even to this day, I hurt in silence about death. I often think about what life would be like if they were still here. I'm still human, and I hurt when death occurs.

"I will forever love my Aunt Lonnie, and again, you are now in my second book. I hope you're proud of my journey and my life because I am proud of you for just being you. Your life wasn't easy, but you lived it to the fullest. I know you're resting. I miss you. Death isn't easy, but it's your truth. Keep watching down on us like I know you always do."

Love, **Nina**

I strongly believe it. If I had to describe the "past" in one word, it would be: defining. It shaped the woman I am. It didn't always feel good while I was going through it, but looking back now, every scar came with a lesson. Every failure became a foundation. And every mistake— yes, even the ones I swore I'd never recover from— became a part of my testimony.

There's something powerful about growth that comes from pain. It's the kind of growth you can't get from comfort. I used to feel ashamed about how many times I had to learn the hard way, but now I don't. I'm proud of that girl. Because she kept getting back up. She didn't always know who she was, but she knew she didn't want to stay broken. That girl kept showing up for herself, even when the world was too heavy. And that same spirit lives in me today.

The truth is, I was raised in a world where silence covered everything. You didn't talk about your struggles; you just survived them. But I made a promise to myself: I would not raise my daughters that way. I would teach them that strength isn't silence, it's honesty. It's saying, "I'm not okay, and I will still try again tomorrow." It's telling you the truth so nobody else gets stuck in theirs.

That's why I speak so boldly now. Not because I'm healed, but because I'm healing— and I want that same freedom for them.

What people don't always understand is: when you're a mother who's been through hell, you don't just raise children, you raise warriors. You raise protectors. You raise little women who know their worth because you finally started learning yours. And even on the days when I was unsure of myself, I was never uncertain of the kind of women I wanted them to be: bold, compassionate, wise, and fearless. I don't pretend to have all the answers. There are still days when life knocks me off balance, and I have to find my footing all over again. But I always do.

I've learned how to ground myself. Whether that's through prayer, journaling, crying in the shower, or taking a walk and talking to God out loud, I find my way back to myself every single time. And I want you, the reader, to know: you are not weak for feeling deeply. You are not broken because life has broken you. You are just human. And there is still so much life left to live after your lowest moment.

So, take your time. Be soft with yourself. And when it gets too loud in the world, go inward. God still hears the whispers of your soul. I've lost people I thought I could never live without. I've had days when I didn't know how I'd make it— financially, emotionally, and mentally. But God kept me. Even when I doubted Him, even when I yelled at the sky with tears in my eyes, He held me through it. And every time I thought I had reached the end of myself, He showed me there was more. More strength. More grace. More purpose.

My past may not have been perfect, but it was necessary. Every chapter. Every loss. Every breakdown. It all brought me here. And here is a place I never thought I'd reach, but I'm so glad I did. So if you're in your "past" right now— if your present feels like pain and you don't see a way out— hold on. Keep going. Let this part of my story remind you that better doesn't always come quickly, but it always comes.

You got this just like I did!

PURPOSE

PURPOSE: Part I

Okay, enough of that.... *Life After Better Days* keeps getting better, and as I write, I feel relieved to share my story without feeling judged, talked about, or lied to.

Honestly, I don't care about that. In society today, some people look at others' lives and want to live it, not me. My life was written out for a reason, and I wouldn't want it any other way. I feel like that's why I don't watch a lot of TV, because all television is fake or is designed to program your mind or be in competition with people you don't even know. THAT IS NOT YOUR PURPOSE in life, so erase that out of your thought process.

Live your life and run your own race. Stay in your own lane at your own pace. Never look at someone's life and say you want your life to be like theirs. Create your own story and inspire someone. Let them know your struggles and the good times in your journey. Life isn't always good, and that's how the world has become accustomed. I don't know about you, but I'm okay with waiting a little longer for what I deserve. I don't want anything just handed to me. I want to work for everything I have.

I realized that as I got older, my thoughts are what make me so unique. My calling and purpose in life is to motivate and inspire just about anyone who's willing to listen and understand life, so my go-to would be just reading and writing.

I love to feed my mind with knowledge so that I can pass it on to the best of my ability. I'm old school, so I write a lot of things down, but I also have a photogenic brain and can remember a lot. What I also do to ease my mind is listen to music, and I mean, all genres. Let me really love and listen to a song, and with the brain I have, I will literally pick the whole song apart. I like to figure out why the artist made the song because whether you know it or not, writers and artists run hand in hand. They have to write down what they're thinking about, and they eventually make it into a song.

With writers, they express and write down how they feel and turn it into a book, article, and so forth. I also know that some people aren't good at expressing themselves verbally, so they'll listen to a song and send it to the person they want to talk to. The song will be full-blown about the topic of conversation they wanted to have and couldn't. TRUST me, there is always a message in music.

Life works out from all different angles. My message is to stop comparing your life to others. Instead of trying to compete with others, let your competition be strictly on you and who you used to be up until now. You'll never feel alive if you seek confirmation and validation from others. Being your authentic self is all you need; it's not defined by your profession, but by your talents, skills, and wisdom. This comes from always remembering your purpose in life and moving forward. Everyday life... sheesh! I say this proudly because life is life, and if you don't have the mindset, it'll have you sinking.

Now, there is no such thing as a "PERFECT LIFE," but you can try to live as comfortably as possible. Stand for SOMETHING or fall for ANYTHING! With that being said, loyalty runs hand in hand with standing up for yourself. The definition of loyalty is: A strong feeling of support or allegiance.

A person's devotion or sentiment of attachment to a particular object. Even at a young age, I was loyal. It was in me, not on me, 35 years, almost 36 years later. I stand on loyalty; I love hard, so my loyalty has to match. But I want to let you know what I've learned over the years: be loyal, but not stupid. Some people see how loyal you are and use it against you just to see how far you'll go for them. You're like prey to their vicious ways.

I had to learn to really read a person, and to my surprise, I was right. Don't get me wrong, stay solid, but watch who you invest your loyalty in. Cut ties with love from a distance and keep the ones who share your loyalty close. Don't walk around looking for people to do you wrong; instead, let things take time, and eventually, the truth will be revealed. That's where knowing yourself comes into play. You must know what you'll tolerate or won't.

Purpose isn't something you stumble upon; it's something you grow into over time. Sometimes it feels like life throws so many distractions and detours your way that you forget why you're here. But when you slow down and listen to your own heart — not the noise of the world — that's when your true purpose begins to shine through.

I've learned that purpose is deeply personal. It's not about what others expect from you or the shiny things society tells you to chase. Your purpose is the quiet voice inside, urging you to keep going, to keep creating, and to keep showing up even on the days when everything feels heavy. It's the part of you that finds meaning in your struggles and transforms them into strength.

There's power in owning your story and being unapologetic about it. When you share your journey, your victories, and your setbacks, you create space for others to do the same. That's how we build communities — not by pretending life is perfect, but by embracing the messy, beautiful reality of it all.

And here's the truth I've come to embrace: your path won't look like anyone else's, and that's a good thing. It means you get to write your own rules and define success on your own terms. Comparison will only steal your joy and leave you chasing shadows. Instead, turn your eyes inward. Reflect on how far you've come, what you've learned, and who you want to become.

This journey is about self-love and self-respect. It's about setting boundaries that protect your peace and choosing loyalty, but only to those who uplift and respect you in return. You don't owe anyone your energy, especially if they don't value it. Learning to say no, to walk away, and to protect your heart is one of the strongest acts of purpose you can perform. Keep moving forward, one step at a time, with intention and clarity. Fill your mind with knowledge, your soul with music, and your heart with courage. Let your life be a testament to resilience, authenticity, and unwavering loyalty — not just to others, but most importantly, to yourself.

Remember, purpose isn't a destination — it's a daily commitment to living fully and truly. And if you stay on that path,

Life After Better Days will be exactly what you make it: a life of meaning, growth, and endless possibilities. One of the most important lessons I've learned on this journey is that purpose isn't static— it evolves as you evolve. What feels like your calling today might shift tomorrow, and that's okay.

Life is fluid and so should be your approach to your dreams and goals. The key is to stay connected to your core values and what feels authentic to you.

Too often, people get caught up trying to live someone else's version of success or happiness. They chase fame, money, or approval without ever asking themselves if those things truly satisfy their soul. But the real purpose feeds you from the inside out. It gives you energy when you're drained and hope when the world feels heavy. It helps you make choices that align with your truth instead of what looks good on paper or pleases others.

I want you to understand that your worth is not measured by what you have or what you achieve, it's measured by how well you know yourself and how fiercely you protect your peace. It takes courage to walk away from toxic relationships, to say no to opportunities that don't feel right, and to stand firm when others doubt you. But that courage is part of your purpose, too. It's what shapes your character and builds your legacy.

Music, writing, and reading aren't just hobbies for me. They are lifelines. They help me process emotions, learn new perspectives, and connect with others on a deeper level. Whether it's a lyric that speaks to my soul or a page in a book that shifts my mindset. These moments of connection remind me that I am not alone and that there is beauty even in pain. I encourage you to find your own outlets, whatever helps you stay centered and inspired.

Maybe it's art, dance, prayer, or simply quiet moments in nature. Whatever it is, nurture it. Let it be the fuel that keeps your spirit burning bright.

Lastly, I want to remind you: It's okay to take your time. Life isn't a race or a competition. It's your unique story unfolding day by day. Celebrate your progress, no matter how small it may seem. Every step forward is a victory. Every lesson learned is a gift. So when you feel overwhelmed or discouraged, remember why you started. Remember that your life, with all its ups and downs, is meaningful. You have a purpose that no one else can fulfill because you are one of a kind. And that is something truly powerful. Keep shining. Keep growing. Keep believing in yourself. I had to work on these throughout my years of dating:

1. Caring too much -Yes, I always cared about others' feelings and never about mine. Men can sense that and take advantage.

2. Treating a man like your child instead of your spouse - I always had that motto that if I got it, you got it, and I still believe in that, but some men/women take that and never do anything with their life and expect you to be their mother. DON'T BE FOOLED BY HELPING AND MOTHERING BIG DIFFERENCE!!!! This can go for males or females.

3. Another thing I also did was sit with a person who knew the streets better than anyone I've ever known in my life, Dom, and asked his opinion. I told him to give me his point of view about this life.

He went on and started by saying, "Soulja Sis, you're too loyal and nice. Men can smell that and take full advantage. Some men want a good woman, and some men just want straight trash."

He also said to me, "You nag too much, lol. Niggas don't be wanting to hear that all the time."

But I jumped in to say, "I nag because I care and want to see the best for him, especially if I love him."

"But that's where you need to back off because if they want it bad enough, they'll go out and get it."

He also said that's where it draws the line from girlfriend to trying to be his mother.

He continued, "Some men/women don't like to see their spouse doing better than them, meaning if you are doing more than them, if you are doing better than your significant other, they will find someone beneath them to make them feel like a man."

He even went on to say that some men just don't deserve a good woman because they're scared, but some need that support to balance them out. I considered all that and found myself a lot happier, but I still needed more knowledge. I'm all for feeding myself with input and ideas that can better my life and relationships, especially if you believe it will work. This goes for men and women. I never want any of my readers to think I don't prefer just one gender: this goes for male and female.

Relationships should never come easily, like okay we meet, we're happy, committed, and trusting each other, etc. "NO," there will be bumps in the road. Never speak off emotions. You can hurt yourself and others because of you being angry. So let me wrap this part of love up:

Ladies/Guys, if you really love each other, it's meant to be worked out. There's a journey ahead of any relationship, but to stand by your spouse is everything. If you work together, it should never be a one-sided thing because you will always fall short. Try not to always think negatively! Never play dumb either; love takes time. Don't rush. Your main goals should be *Better Days*.

Moving forward, you'll know what's right for you if you just stand still and let it come to you, and if it's worth fighting for, do just that. If not, walk away. You know what you'll tolerate and won't. I have spent a lot of my years making people happy, WRONG!! That was my truth; fast forward to the grown woman I am today, I can't make anyone happy because it should come from within. Meaning you have to create that for yourself, even with my daughters.

I always tell them: You are only responsible for your happiness, no one else's. It's your day, and everyone has the same 24 hours. How they choose to spend it has nothing to do with you. It's ultimately up to them to set the tone on their own life and vice versa. So, don't miss out on your happiness because one isn't. To break it down a little more.... The whole concept I'm trying to get to is that you're not responsible for anyone's moods but yours. I know it probably sounds harsh, but this is my TRUTH and how I live my life. The truth hurts if you don't understand it.

We often pretend to be happy with ourselves with a lie! In reality, the truth hurts. But to be honest, I would rather hurt and heal from a situation, even if it's being revealed and it crushes me to the core.

I had a situation going on in my life and I spoke to my mom about it and she stated - I quote, "Nina, it's better that you tell the truth about it."

That right there made me look at honesty and the truthfulness of life. I always hated hurting people's feelings, but that goes back to what I previously said, "IT'S not your feelings." My whole purpose is never to destroy a person but to be candid. So, back then, I would tell the truth but put a little spin on it. Now, it's like I'm as blunt as ever. You are going to get the truth and nothing but the truth. As long as the air is clear, you've done your part.

Always be open to listening to others as well and consider what they have to say. Communication is everything. Give whoever is speaking the chance to tell their truth as well, without getting angry or trying to pressurize others. My purpose is mainly everything I went through after my PAST and PAIN stages, and I'm here to tell you that it can repeat cycles.

You can have a purpose in life, but the pain of something occurs, and now you're stuck in that moment, or you can be in pain about something or a certain situation or scenario and get triggered about your past. Do not beat yourself up about going backward. That's the beauty of life. It just sharpens you up so that you can be stronger than the last time.

I'm a firm believer in second chances. You just have to learn from your mistakes and make every lesson a learning experience. A prime example is when I see repeated clients come into the facility; many of them will see me and instantly put their heads down. Nope!!! When I see them, I just feel happy that they made it back to try again and to do it the right way. This goes round.

The journey is always hard, but to make an effort and do all you can do. The attempt is the most amazing part. Another thing that I wanted to speak on is being at war with yourself. I definitely suffered from this as well. I promise you, my purpose in life was to go through my way of life so that I can be a vessel to others. I always knew I was different, but in this world, it's easy to get distracted by anything that can disconnect you from your purpose.

An interference or disturbance of any kind can knock you off your game, whether it's a job, friendships, or even a relationship. Most importantly, you can be your worst enemy, meaning you're distracting yourself just by having negative thoughts. So let me explain, you're in a dead-end job, but you know you deserve better. You serve a different purpose, but you settle for many reasons. You are at war with yourself because you know you want better, right?

My advice to my readers is to rectify your situation. Work hard to get out of that job, but learn from that dead-end job. It doesn't always have to be a bad adventure with you, working there. Your journey doesn't stop just at that job, especially when it's the bare minimum of what you

deserve.

One of the hardest battles I fought was learning to care for myself as much as I cared for others. It's so easy to pour your heart into someone else, hoping it will fix things, heal wounds, or keep the relationship alive. But over time, I realized that neglecting my feelings was doing more harm than good.

Loving yourself isn't selfish; it's necessary. When you don't love yourself enough, you'll allow others to treat you less than you deserve. That's a lesson that cost me a lot of tears and heartbreak, but I'm grateful for it now.

And yes, treating a partner like your child instead of your equal is a trap many fall into. I used to think taking care of someone meant being their everything— mom, cheerleader, and provider of comfort. But that dynamic isn't healthy. Real partnership means growth on both sides. You give support, yes, but you don't become a crutch or a replacement for their own responsibility. Sometimes, love means stepping back and letting the other person face their own battles. That's tough, but it's necessary for true respect and equality.

Love isn't always a fairy tale. It takes work, patience, and a lot of honest communication. There will be fights, misunderstandings, and moments when you question everything. However, if the foundation is strong, you continue to build. If not, it's okay to walk away without guilt. Knowing your worth means you don't settle for less than what nourishes your soul.

Talking to someone who's been through the streets opened my eyes even more. Loyalty and kindness are beautiful, but in the wrong hands, they can be used against you. It's heartbreaking to admit, but some people seek out the good-hearted just to tear them down or control them. That conversation made me realize the importance of protecting my spirit, setting boundaries, and learning when to say no, even if my heart wanted to say yes.

I also had to face the reality that not everyone will celebrate your success. Sometimes, when you're shining, others feel threatened or left behind. That insecurity can make them act out or push you away. It's painful, but I learned that your progress is not their problem— it's yours to own and embrace proudly. Don't dim your light to make others comfortable. Keep shining.

Truth and honesty became my pillars, even when it hurt. Sugarcoating reality only delays healing. I learned to be straightforward with myself and others because clarity brings peace. Sometimes the truth stings, but it clears the air and allows growth. That's why I always encourage open communication, listen without judgment and speak without fear.

When pain from your past tries to pull you back, remember it's not failure. It's a reminder that you're still human and in the process of healing. Don't shame yourself for setbacks. Every time you get back up, you're stronger than before.

Second chances aren't just for fairy tales— they're real, and they're necessary. Life isn't linear, and sometimes we have to circle back, try again, and do better. What matters is that you never give up on yourself.

Being at war with yourself is exhausting, but you can choose peace. If your current life isn't what you dreamed of, don't settle. Work hard, learn the lessons, but keep your eyes on the prize— your purpose. Don't let fear or frustration derail your path. Your journey is uniquely yours, filled with ups and downs, lessons and victories. Embrace it all. The pain, the joy, the setbacks— they're shaping you into the person you're meant to be.

And that person? They're worth every struggle and every step forward. I also say that, in any case of being at war with yourself, you could become emotionally drained just by settling for the job, friendship, or relationship that you don't want to be in—

for example, mending friendships that serve you no purpose and what you want in life.

I had recently read an article about soldiers during a war, and it stated that eighty percent of soldiers don't call their families because it's a distraction; the minute they do, it can be deadly because their minds are thinking about other things. It's unbalanced and not focused on what it needs to be focused on. I honestly agree with that because if I were at war with one of my soldiers, I wouldn't trust my life to be secure with them if they had so much on their mind that they couldn't protect their fellow men or women. You can't be distracted in certain environments; it just won't work. You can be killed.

My suggestion for anyone is not to let life get to you, and trust me, it will. Your mind has to be stronger than your body. It's so easy for your flesh to be weak, but your mind has to stay sharp. I have been in so many positions in life that I felt like I was losing my mind. I wasn't even competent in what was going on around me.

It was absolutely the power of prayer that got me through. You have to learn how to take the good with the bad and let life flow so that you won't drive yourself crazy with doubts, fears, or even things that happened to you. I didn't think my life would be like this.

Another reason why I felt at war with myself and misunderstood is because of how I struggled with a lot of things as a teenager. I struggled with not having my biological father around, my love addiction with boys/men, drugs, alcohol, school, and my preference of sex relationships, you name it. It gets hard when you're not understood the right way by certain people.

Some of the reasons why people look at me differently and as weirdly was because they are judgmental and love to see you down. That's their way of picking themselves up, not knowing that a person that feels misunderstood just needs a listening ear and a closed mouth. They also need someone that will understand or even someone who has been in that situation who can give them some advice.

After high school, I dealt with a lot, but I made it through with graduating, but I also struggled with whether I wanted to date a man or a woman? Yup, I was curious, and I kept it inside for a long time until I sat my mom down and told her that I have an interest in girls. That phase didn't last long at all. LOL! It just wasn't my thing, but as soon as it got out, that was the headline of my family and friends.

Nobody even asked me why? What motivated you to try it out? Nothing! They just bashed me. Few of them wouldn't even talk to me. Even in arguments, I would get ripped apart. They didn't even realize that it was a cry for help. NOT ATTENTION but for HELP! I was going to go my way regardless, but it didn't make it any better for people to misunderstand me either.

I came to the conclusion that those who judge you are often those who are not happy with themselves. As I grew older, I realized that it's a shame, but it's all true. Now I look back on my life and thank God that I was misunderstood and fighting a war within my body. It made me stronger, so I can tell my story without care in the world or worry about who will judge me.

I'm just thankful that I'm alive to share my story and help the next generation. Sometimes, a person needs a stronger person to come forward and tell their story so they can gather the courage to tell theirs. "To misunderstand is to fail to interpret or understand the words or actions of someone's corrections."

If you are the person who judges others and fails to understand them, just listen because everyone is going through a struggle. I was able to cope with being misunderstood. A lot of people can't, and they go downhill, even turning to suicide. Being misunderstood begins and ends with your mind running too fast. Yes! It runs even when you're sleeping. Yes, it's hard to believe, but for me, I was thinking while I was sleeping.

I remember talking to my mother about how my brain runs fast while I'm asleep, and she said, "Nina, you're not at peace."

At first, I was like, 'Okay, Mom, whatever you say,' but then, as I sat back and observed my life, I could say I wasn't. I'm not exactly where I want to be in life, but for everything I stress about, there is always a positive side too. So, I try not to stress.

Life can be a lot harder, and it can be a lot easier. It's just the way you live it. But even after I reevaluated my life, my brain wouldn't let me just get a break, so I figured I would write a book and just put my heart and soul into it. Like I said, there's a positive side to your brain working overtime, but there's also a negative side.

When I first experienced what I'm about to tell you, it scared me. One day, my brain was on overload for about two weeks straight, maybe longer. Now, that means once again, even when I was asleep, my brain was still working. So, it's like interfering with my sleeping pattern. Anyway, I remember it was a Friday.

At work, I remember feeling like my brain was going to explode. Sure enough, I went to get my girls from the after-school program, and I forgot where I was supposed to take them for the weekend. I'm so glad I got them there in the time that I did. I hopped back into my truck and looked in the rearview mirror, and my eyes were bloodshot red. I made it home and fell asleep. I could not wake up. I lie to you not. I woke up Sunday morning.

On Friday, my brain crashed. It was like I was dead; I had no control over my body. I just never wanted that to happen to me while I was with my girls. It's scary, so I try my hardest to just take life one day at a time. I still suffer from my brain working too much, but what I do know is really try and block things out.

Sometimes it works and sometimes it doesn't. I pray more than ever. I pray over my thoughts. I really do pray because without prayer, there's no healing. I don't know where I would be. I pray for my sanity and I also meditate, and to do that, you have to be in tune with yourself. You have to block out everything social media, television, people, and things.

What I do when I start my meditation when I'm in deep thought and need to come back to realization is I cut my phone, computer, lights, and whatever else can distract me. It works. Please try to consider that even if you must cry it out, letting the tears out is a cleanser. I wanted people to know the real "me" so that they can understand that you're not alone in any situation. My eyes are open to many things. Don't get me wrong; I'm still in a struggle, and I go through everyday situations. I just know how to cope and live.

Life is all about how you make it. I know that people live for the future, and yes, that's a good way of living. I just try to live day by day, with nothing promised. The definition of a journey is an act of traveling from one place to another. I've experienced many things in my life, both good and bad. My journey was tough, but I persevered and made it through.

To dance in the rain, you must first learn to praise him in the storm. I danced in the rain plenty of times on my journey, but as a soldier at war, I always kept God first through it all and still do to this day. That's very important! Keep your head high and try not to sink. Don't suffocate your life because you only have one life to live. Always aim to heal and move on from ANY situation.

I just hope that I was able to support and uplift someone in need. I laid my life's highlights on the line in hopes that I could get through to someone who is going through anything that you read in the *Life After Better Days*. I feel like I've stepped out of my comfort zone, being a private person, and today, you can finally start to put the pieces together.

And most importantly, start to live. Breath! It's okay. Inhale and exhale.

Love, *Nina*

-Guilt-

A lot has happened since I put the pen down for a minute. Okay, so where do I start? So many people I love are suffering rather from love, trauma, drugs, death, etc. So, I touch on those in particular.

Now, these all run hand in hand for some, and if it doesn't relate, don't take offense, just help someone if you do know a person in need. Love can be a beautiful thing when it's handled properly. That goes for family, friends, relationships, whatever, or whoever you love. But it is abused as well.

I personally have the biggest heart, it's way too big for this life and world we live in. I take it so seriously. I think it comes with the trauma I endured. I went through trauma at a young age, and to be honest, I wouldn't take anything back, and I mean absolutely NOTHING!!!

I sometimes think if I didn't go through the childhood trauma, would I have a lot to say? Would I be the motivational, inspiring, free-spirited person that I am? I was always curious to know that answer. I was destined to be great. I know that for a fact.

My trauma wants to destroy me, many use trauma to sit in their darkness so that they won't have to deal with life, and in a way, I can honestly say that I did so.

On July 18th, 2023, I was crushed by life. My dad, my protector, left me and crossed over to the other side (heaven). It made me feel unlit on the inside. I can touch on this because it's still fresh, and I'm still going through the motions of his eternal rest.

My dad's departure from life was sudden. I always knew he suffered from the loss of his hearing and his childhood traumas, even the death of his first-born son. He endured many things before he was finally able to rest.

But when I look at it, his soul is free. Now, that's the numbness talking because grief is a full circle of emotions. I wouldn't be me if I didn't reveal to y'all my truth. I am angry, hurt, and depressed. I cry and scream, I talk to myself a lot just to get out what I'm thinking and want to actually say. The real reason why I'm so hurt is because I feel like my dad wasn't supposed to leave us.

I know people aren't forever, but my story is different. He loved me, and without him, I wouldn't have known how it felt to be loved! So, this pain is deep. Life goes on, and I understand, but now, I am going through the motions of grieving. I'm at the GUILT PART.

I'm a realist, and so many people know that about me; this is both a gift and a curse. I say whatever or however I feel. My dad died alone, and he died heartbroken (Just my opinion.) The guilt comes into play because we could have done more and celebrated life with him just a little bit more.

My siblings and I loved our dad so much, and we celebrated his life with him, but it just wasn't enough. Let me elaborate, people tend to celebrate death more than life; that's the most terrible programmed way of thinking. They should have or would have been at an all-time high with guilt.

I remember when my dad was alive; he would blow up my phone on Facebook Messenger just to see my face and talk to me.

He was lonely. I answered many of his calls, and there were times when I didn't. I might have been busy or just going through my own adult life.

He honestly just wanted to talk. He talked a lot, LOL. Even if he was drunk, just seeing his children made his day. I could remember many of his birthdays. We used to get him a cake, beer, food, and liquor, and just go over to his high-rise and enjoy his birthday with him. We NEVER neglected him, so don't get that picture. We just could have done better, and this is just my take on it.

Life has its way of being, and for me, the guilt makes me cringe because I'd do anything right now to be able to take that ride on the North Side to pick him up and ride around the city with him, LOL. I also look at life from many different aspects. Our brother got murdered nine and a half months before our father passed, and they didn't have the best relationship. It wasn't because of either of their doings, so I look at it as if we had our dad, and now it's Benny's turn.

This too shall pass was what I kept saying to myself, but my flesh was so weak. I was screaming, but no one could hear me. I felt like the world was moving, and I was standing still, like I was in the Twilight Zone. Guilt is unbearable. It puts you at a discomfort that you hate to be in, but as each day goes on, I'm learning not to be so selfish about the fact that our father's life has ended, and now he can rest. It will never be easy for us, so give us time to let it all soak in.

For me, the GUILT is seeping in, and I have to go through it to grow through it. Losing my brother, Lil Dante, just nine and a half months before losing my dad felt like the ground beneath me was being pulled out twice in rapid succession. Each loss carried its own kind of pain, but together, they formed a storm that nearly drowned me.

Dante's death was sudden, violent, and shattered the family in ways words can't fully capture. Our relationship wasn't perfect— there was tension and hurt, like in any family, but losing him was like losing a part of myself. There's a hole left behind when a sibling passes; a connection that's both blood and history is suddenly broken. It wasn't just about grief — it was about unfinished conversations, missed chances, and the rawness of life stopped too soon.

I try to remind myself that we loved them. That we celebrated their lives while they were here as best as we could, even if it never feels like it was enough. But grief has a way of making you question everything, including the love you gave. The truth is, grief and guilt don't follow a timeline. They don't fade in neat ways. Sometimes, the guilt makes me feel frozen— like I'm stuck in a moment where the world moves on but I'm trapped in a twilight zone of pain.

But I'm learning, slowly, that guilt isn't a punishment— it's a sign of how deeply you loved. And with that love comes the responsibility to forgive yourself. We must understand that grief is a journey without a map, and that healing doesn't mean forgetting but carrying their memory with grace. It means holding onto the lessons they taught me, the love they gave me, and using that to find strength even in the darkest moments.

Losing Lil' Dante and our dad, back-to-back, was one of the hardest things I've ever faced. But their lives, their love, and even their pain remind me that I am still here— still fighting to grow, to heal, and to live a life that honors them both.

Guilt is a complicated emotion. It sneaks in when you least expect it and sticks around longer than you want. After losing someone as close as a father, the guilt can feel overwhelming, like a weight that you carry on your shoulders every single day. I've come to understand that guilt often comes from love. It's the part of you that wishes you had done more, been more, said more.

It's the voice that whispers 'what if?' Whispering over and over until it becomes a roar. What if I had answered every call? What if I had spent more time with him? What if I had been there when he needed me most? But here's the thing: guilt doesn't change the past. It only steals your peace in the present.

Grief and guilt are intertwined— they feed off each other in a way that can trap you in a cycle of pain. But I've learned the hard way that you've to allow yourself to feel these emotions fully, because trying to suppress them only makes them fester and louder. You have to face the guilt head-on, like staring into a mirror that reflects your deepest fears and regrets. And yet, amid all that pain, there's a lesson. A lesson about compassion, especially self-compassion.

We are human, and human beings make mistakes. We get distracted by life, by our own struggles, and sometimes we miss the moments that truly matter. But that doesn't mean love wasn't there, and it certainly doesn't mean that the person we lost didn't know how much we cared.

Guilt can teach you to appreciate life more fiercely— to celebrate the living, not just the dead. Because too often, as I said, people wait until someone is gone to celebrate them, when the real magic happens when they're still here to hear it. If I could tell anyone walking through grief right now one thing, it would be this: forgive yourself.

Forgive yourself for the missed calls, the busy days, and the times you weren't perfect. Forgive yourself because you loved deeply and imperfectly, and that's all anyone can ask for. And while the pain of losing someone will never fully go away, you can learn to carry it differently. You can carry it as a reminder of the love you shared, not as a burden of what you didn't do.

In time, the guilt will lose its grip. It will soften into bittersweet memories and lessons learned. And through that process, you will grow stronger, kinder, and more present— not just for yourself, but for those you love. Because at the end of the day, guilt is just a feeling. Feel it, learn from it, and then let it go. That's how we heal. That's how we honor those we've lost.

Moving along after our dad's passing, I made some major changes in my life because of what I endured and had to accept after his casket closed. I worked in drug and alcohol, so I see a lot. I accomplished a tremendous amount of things in the facility where I was employed, from mopping floors and wiping beds to being a motivational and inspirational speaker who saved lives.

I was at the center of the room with women and men who were addicted. I placed the clients in outpatient/inpatient services and watched the people come in and out. I spoke life into anyone who wanted to listen and make a change. I truly believe that whatever I go through is a blessing, and I always want to shed light on anyone.

The reason I'm saying all of this is that I have a voice, and many do not. I stand on what comes out of my mouth. Even if I haven't been through it, I'm used to giving a person a boost of my vibrant energy and guiding them to those who have been in their current situation. Working in a facility, you have to have tough skin. Especially when you are dealing with the same things and people you see outside of work with the people you love the most. That is where it hit home for me.

I was never or will never be embarrassed by anyone who was addicted, whether it was a family member, lover, friend, etc. I have decided to step aside so that I can assist them individually and privately. In my head, I always thought, *How can I speak to people I don't even know at work and pour life into them in groups... when my own loved ones are struggling?* It was just emotional, to say the least. The guilt ate me up so much that I left three months after my dad passed. Was it the smartest decision I made? I'm not sure, but anything that helps a person is up my alley. It's not a job; it's a lifestyle. I didn't ask for this gift. I was born with it.

I scare myself sometimes because of my thought process. I'm teachable and love to teach those who are willing. I read and listen to podcasts. I try to stay in tune with people who are speaking about beneficial things that I can learn from. I truly believe that some conversations have no purpose in listening to a brain like mine. Some individuals become upset and angry at a high-spirited person for several reasons.

I won't dwell on pity for too long, so if I'm having a conversation with someone while they're speaking to me about anything, especially a problem, my mind is running on how they can come up with a solution to what is being presented to me. Along with strategizing the plot and the plan, I never belittle anyone. That's not my way of helping a person by beating them down or judging. I just want to help as much as I can and be a vessel to someone in need. Even if my life is at a standstill, strength comes from experience, so the guilt I endured will make me become the woman I once was in due time because *Life After Better Days* has become tremendously harder for me.

The temptation of loving myself and others was slim to none. I was hurting and drowning in guilt and grief. I wanted people to be there for me how I was there for them. I came to the conclusion that life doesn't work in that order. Respectfully, I always see situations from every aspect. As the months passed, I realized that some may not be reaching out for the same reason; they are still fighting battles and grieving from whatever life throws at them, but I was angry and furious. Some deal with death and trauma differently!

As 2024 approached, I became someone I couldn't recognize in some ways. I love the woman I was becoming, but I was also afraid. The world pressures you to change, and I'm totally against that. Do things when you feel the need to change, never let anyone be so demanding about what you know you need to work on. Even if it takes you 365 days ten times, let it not wear failure on your shoulders. And when you accomplish a goal or a plan, honor your past self for getting you through. Always remember: a little progress is better than no progress; each day adds up to big results. Never think it's not noticed, or you didn't do enough. Continue to build.

Every day can be a beautiful beginning or a painful struggle.

A wise friend once told me, "That you can't put too much on a person, it becomes entitlement, and no one is entitled to feel the way you feel or even understand."

Talking about an eye opener, that statement alone opened my eyes up. It's extremely important to know that the quicker you change your mindset and train yourself to think that way, the easier your life will be. I now understand that people come into your life for a reason, a season, and a lifetime.

Lastly, a feeling refers to experiencing something physical or emotional, such as a traumatic occurrence or situation. If an individual has never endured the pain of losing a parent, what can they really say to me? Even if their pain is different, it's humanly impossible for another individual to tell another person that they "Know what they are going through" because it's a lie.

You don't because I DON'T. We have to just somehow still get up every day and walk through LIFE even if your loved ones have gone to their afterlife.

After my dad's passing and my drinking heavily, I decided to journal, just to somehow navigate through life. On that first day, I started journaling.

↔

January 8, 2024 (PAIN)

I woke up feeling stagnant. I would say I don't know why, but I do. From October to March, I'm literally in grind and survival mode. It seems like everything that I think can go wrong does. From bills to my children's birthdays, sibling wars, jobs, my vehicle, just EVERYTHING!!!

I'm literally in a spiritual warfare, y'all. Meaning I'm fighting against all the work of preternatural evil forces. Today I woke up, got the girls ready for school, and after dropping them off, I made breakfast and poured a drink (alcohol). Now, I don't think drinking is bad at all, but I was so lost in my thoughts that I wanted to ease my mind with a drink at 9:00 am. I texted my best friend for a few, and I drifted off to sleep. Woke up with a major headache, but I still got up, showered, and started my day! Now, it's time for me to get my girls from school, and while riding home, my middle daughter was in the car and we briefly were talking about Life After Better Days, and she said, "Mommy, I'm proud of you!"

Quickly after her saying that, I said, "For what baby?" She goes on to say, "Because I didn't think you were going to write another book." I looked at her in the rearview mirror and said, "Mommy works hard and that's cool and all, but I want to leave you and your sisters something more like an accomplishment. I don't think life is all about punching a clock. Yes, that's great and all, but work on something that will leave a lasting legacy - your gift, no matter what it is." She instantly smiled.

I do everything to benefit children; I know ifs, ands, or buts about it. I show and demonstrate real-life examples to each of my daughters. I want them to see their mother succeed.

↔

January 9, 2024 (PURPOSE)

Today I felt rushed.

Has anyone ever had the feeling that their life just moves way too fast? I got to work a couple of minutes late, so I was behind. There was a two-hour delay, so the girls were home, but it left me in a panic, just having to worry about them going outside while I'm at work, to go to school. This was fine, but I just always think about how my youngest feels. It's really an unexplainable thought. She's so young and just doesn't know she's so strong for her size, and she follows her sisters and me. Aa'Layah amazes me every day.

Moving along in my day, I went to work, and one of my favorite coworkers said something at the end of our work shift that had me on edge. Now, by no means am I making excuses for myself. I ran a little late or behind to work. It can be anywhere from 2-5 minutes late, I'll admit. But I execute every time, not to mention I am breaking down walls from my previous employment because

102

I had a lot of leeway, which means I had a lot of freedom to do things without facing any consequences or restrictions!

Nonetheless, she mentioned how I should go and talk to my supervisor about my time, but she followed up with, "Also, tell her how you are a single mother and how you don't have a husband at home to help you with your daughters." If looks could kill, her ass would have been dead.

However, what I did was clock out and simply said, "Well, let me leave so I can get my daughters together for school tomorrow and not be late anymore."

↔

I'm only sharing this message with you, as my reader, because I could have snapped at her for stereotyping me. I had to take a deep breath. I was proud of myself because I talked to her here and there about being a mother of three and how I raised them by myself.

So, I couldn't be mad; you literally have to watch what you say to humans. After I went home, I spoke to my daughters, and of course, we came up with a plan to do better. We are not perfect and never will be, but trying is all that we can do, and that is all that matters. I decided to journal for my readers so you can get a glimpse of some of my everyday normal, as though I'm living *Life After Better Days*.

People tend to want to live this fairytale life. I don't, nor do I care to live my life. It's golden. Going through life lessons has gotten me this far, and it carries my faith, strength, and ability to keep going. It should be the same for you as well. If you care about what people or a person thinks of you, you'll always try to live based on another's perception. Stop that! Do it for your own sake.

I knew I was running behind on certain days, but now I realize I needed to change my morning routine, possibly even my nighttime routine, to lighten my load. I look at situations from all angles. I move forward to be able to come out on top, even if I have to go through pain. What did you learn from it? It's now a lesson to create your past and walk in your divine purpose.

-Self-Reflection (PAIN PAST PURPOSE)-

Six months of my dad being gone, and what came to mind was *self-reflection*. I'm not sure why, but I just felt the need to speak on it. For those who are unfamiliar with the definition, I'll explain. Self is "You."

Reflection involves taking the time to think about, meditate on, elevate, and give serious thought to your behaviors, attitudes, motivations, and desires. I've been holding on to a lot of salutations that served me no purpose, but they were all negative, and I didn't like that for myself. Everything seemed so cloudy, and I couldn't see the bigger picture or what was right in front of me.

In my books, I always want to motivate and inspire, but how can I ever do that if I'm not following what I teach? Taking a step back from things can be tough, but you have to rebuild, restart, and refocus on your life. That's just what I did, and I feel great to know that I let people, places, and things proceed without my existence. My growth is so real. Things that bothered me no longer exist in my world. *Life After Better Days* was, and still is, an adventure to me because you just never know how your day will turn out.

Self-reflection: I can touch on this topic for days. Its beauty gives me life for so many reasons. My ability to witness my flaws and take accountability is a gift itself. Some don't like to acknowledge their wrong doings. I have to do that so that I can grow as a mother, daughter, sister, niece, friend, co-worker, and entrepreneur.

I love the awareness it puts me on a natural high. Having self-conversations isn't bad. "Check Yourself." Meditation is huge for me. I sit in the dark and shut the world out so that I can think. It feels so refreshing. Putting things on paper is always my go-to as well, and years later, I'm a successful black woman who made some bad choices in life, but I'm able to stand tall and say that. I wrote two books about the accomplishments I set for myself.

Self-reflection is also the way you discipline yourself. I lack in that area, specifically in the way I respond to situations I work on daily. None of what you read in *Life After Better Days* is made up; everything is real. I needed this platform to let the world know it takes time. Please, don't rush or believe that your life must be the way you see people on social media; all that is fake.

Do you notice that some people don't even mention their failures, but instead talk about what went well or what happened positively in life? That's not the way to go! If I'm going to tell my story, it will be from start to finish, including all the trials and tribulations, as well as my personal growth and flaws. You have to have that mindset to practice self-reflection, and that can be difficult. In my mind, I always remember that I've come too far to let anyone trigger me. Trust me, it's hard if you really know me.

I have sat in my own mess, realizing the situation I put myself in, all my mistakes and bad decisions. The biggest thing I had to do was learn that people don't deserve the full blame and that I was a part of my own destruction. Sitting in it is hard, but forgiving myself was harder. Growth is not linear! You can sit in your mess, but don't ever stay there for too long.

↔

January 10, 2024 (PAST)

Today was a relief. I got to work on time, and it felt great. Although I was tired by 4:00, I pushed through my 12-hour shift. I always encourage people to take the initiative and push their way into life. I have many different people that I talk to and shed light on, but I have a deep affection for women. It was

I couldn't understand a woman's take on things until I was blessed with three daughters. I always and still do love a male's perspective of things and life, but I had to change my narrative a little. I always advise women not to compete with other women. That's the devil's work; I really don't see how you can. I will uplift someone at any time. I've never been a jealous type because what's for me and what's for them is just how it sounds.

My blessings are for me, and their blessings are for them. I'm a firm believer in congratulating a person or people and lifting anyone in their season, even if it's not. Also, live the life you're proud of. Take accountability and responsibility with your chin up and chest out. Even when you have Better Days, you still will experience Life After Better Days. The Question is, "Are you ready to take the next step into a world where you have to take responsibility for your Accountability?"

PURPOSE: Part II

My journaling isn't to "Tell my business," as the new generation says; yet, I have nothing to hide, and everyone has a story to tell. For me, I love to write; that's my outlet, and whatever outlet you have to get through life, whether it's well turned out or not, you have to work on it.

Nobody has it all figured out. Some may turn to an activity or hobby to cope with difficult times. Others turn to drugs and alcohol. When you need to make a better decision, do it. Some take longer than others to get the hang of life, but every step, whether it's small or large, is essential. Never quit. Never give in. Never surrender.

I was speaking with my mom tonight, and in addition to our many conversations, the topic was "living with what you have and being appreciative of what one has," along with not worrying about what social media portrays. I admire my mother for several reasons, and I'm sure that if you read *Life After Better Days*, you'll understand how close my mother and I are. She made so much sense, as she always does, and I came right back to reality.

Carrying a heavy load, it's always a blessing to speak and listen, but most importantly, give feedback to another strong individual.

-Self-Reflection (I Rise)-

Giving up is not an option in my book. Always speak life into YOURSELF:

I RISE! I FALL! I RISE AGAIN!

What I also love about self-reflection is that you can work on yourself at any time. It doesn't have to be an automatic switch. Do what works for your divine purpose.

We always want the best for ourselves, but working on yourself at your own pace is the ultimate goal. Do not beat yourself up but acknowledge that you need the change. It's called a habit, so you want to break the cycle of anything negative.

We often get too overwhelmed because we're worried about reaching the finish line, the end goal, when we need to focus on the journey. That will burn you out. Focus on the small things; it won't happen overnight. The human body doesn't work like that. Put in the work and stay consistent.

Winter is the perfect time for me to reflect on myself. Everyone is different, but for me, I focus more when I'm by myself. I spend most of my time at home with my daughters because I genuinely dislike the cold. So I pray more, meditate, and break down my plans. "New Year's Day" is always January first, not for me. I believe that January falls in the winter when I'm manifesting my life, so when spring arrives, I blossom, and then that officially starts my "NEW YEAR."

Another form of self-reflection is journaling.... This is a major thing that I do. One year, I literally had fines that I had to pay off. I journaled every payment I made after I completed. I went into my backyard and burned every piece of paper that had something to do with the mistakes that led me to having to pay the fines. It was, to me, a self-cleansing experience. Remember, everything starts with YOU. If you're not working on becoming a better person, how can you pour into another human?

You must use a step-by-step formula, even if you need to take a detour to get back on track with fixing your life. Once you've made it halfway through your journey of self-reflection, you will love who you see in the mirror and break these barriers. In all honesty, your life probably isn't even as extreme, and you're beating yourself down, trying to figure out your adjustments.

Think about this: Maybe the journey isn't much about becoming anything. Maybe it's about unbecoming everything that isn't you or for you so you can be who you were meant to be in the first place. I'm saying all of that to say: take life day by day and do a lot of soul searching. It's absolutely fine to miss out on figuring out your life purposes. *Life After Better Days* will push you to become the person you pray for, but it all starts and ends with you. Self-Reflection is EVERYTHING.

↔

January 11, 2024

Journaling My Journey

Today was slow. I woke up, did a short meditation, and then just lay around. I texted a couple of people and didn't get the response I was looking for, which triggered me and took me back to a place where I had fought and prayed my way out of.

Just that fast, I knew I wasn't healed all the way; healing, yes, but what I also realized is that I set high expectations for things and situations when I need to accept people for who they are. In some situations, I put myself into, I already know how the outcome is going to turn out, but I give it a try anyway. Unfortunately, I won't be doing that moving forward. It slows down my thought process and my spiritual growth. I realized that some people, places, and things aren't even worth fighting for.

Fast forward, my day went on. Being a mother is my greatest reward, having been blessed with my first daughter sixteen years ago. I've been on a journey to make and raise my daughters the best way I know how. This particular day, I felt like I let my girls down due to a variety of damaging occurrences that I participated in during my younger years, which I still need to address and learn to live with today. I always speak life into each of my daughters and let them know the ways of life. Today was an emotional rollercoaster, but I'm ready for the ride.

-Healing-

Why do people have to heal from trauma that they didn't cause? I often wondered that too? Think about it: some of us were born into trauma... from the wound your mother may have dealt with while you were growing inside of her and during childbirth, it's been proven that the fetus growing into a baby can feel their mother's emotions, right? So a baby coming into the world may already be dealing with the feelings of their carrier.

Another example can be if, after nine months of a parent doing hard drugs and alcohol the whole pregnancy, your child will come into the world with some of the mother's underlying issues. It's trauma either way it goes. Trauma and healing run hand in hand. You have all these situations you have to heal from and don't even know how. We as people don't even know how to heal because living in trauma is way too easy. You learn to adapt to your thinking and behavior as a result of your trauma, when in all reality, healing is so much better. Imagine the feeling of being free and releasing your mind from all the things that hinder your peace.

As I write this, I become emotional, unlocking my inner feelings, and just being able to help someone else helps me with my own healing. If you find yourself reliving the past, let me try and walk you through healing and burying trauma. Now, by all means, I'm not a therapist, and trust me, I AM NOT HEALED YET!!! I'm healing!

Sometimes, we as people find ourselves wanting to run back to the things that we worked so hard on and broke free from. Don't run backward. Realize it's just your trauma calling you back because it's familiar. It's called living in survival. It has its way of feeling like home, even though it's the farthest thing from it. It's the hardest thing in the world to get up every day and give it one hundred percent when you're dealing with life situations, but who said life would be easy?

For me, I try to stay consistent and motivated when the trauma attacks me because it sleeps inside of me. When your body feels like it's healing, trauma creeps back up and tries to destroy you. Take a step back and take the proper steps so that when the attack hits you, you'll know how to fight through it. That's called healing!

Everything is difficult in the beginning. Keep going. Many things are difficult in the middle but keep going. Some things and situations will never stop being difficult. JUST KEEP GOING! It makes a major difference.

Life After Better Days is my story… Nina's and no one else's. You have to keep in mind that it's very important. Whether it's a journal, a pocket diary, or a book, it's yours, and when your gift is to get the message out, do it by any means. You are unstoppable. I stopped many times. I felt like I stopped writing for good, but I always found a way to resurface. To rise again even after the passing of my father, I'll never be the same, but each time I picked up the pen, I became a little less vulnerable.

Becoming unstoppable is what made me find my power again. I no longer put my book as an expectation, but rather a requirement, respecting my time, being patient, and praying over my thoughts, as well as how I wanted to word everything so that I can motivate and inspire my readers. I keep my word in my era. Your word is your bond. Everything you say, you have to stand on. So, to write another book was always my plan. I just never set a date, and I never set goals. I plan only because life will detour you with so many things, and when that date comes up that you set and you couldn't meet your goals, I know, for me, I beat myself up.

Whatever you are gifted with will never go away; you carry it with you for life. So, no matter how many times you have to start, do it to stay consistent with your thoughts. I say all this because the hardest person I've ever had to forgive was myself.

There are many reasons for this, and that's why my mindset is the way it is. I'm street smart and book smart, and I have common sense, knowing that it puts me in a different bracket. Some may think, *Oh, she thinks she knows it all?* But in all actuality, I just experienced and lived a life that I had no control over. I was born into this, and I learned how to apply and tried not to get discouraged in the process.

Trust me, I'm not trying to convince, persuade, or speak as if my life is perfect. It's far from it. I sin daily. What I am trying to do is help you understand that life happens, no matter what journey you have to navigate. Just do it and live life with no regrets at all.

Over the past year of *Life After Better Days*, I had a lot of alone time, which I utilized to my advantage. For me, in all honesty, I had way too much time, being in my head some days was the ultimate worst, while trying to grieve, cope, and live a normal life. While being strong for myself, my children, and others, life showed me that many people in my circle, or who had been in my circle, had eyes and ears closed when it came to me.

I feel like certain ones just didn't care because again, some really do believe that the strong person has it all figured out. We don't! In all honesty, we just know how to maneuver through life with our head held high. We often just deal with life situations on our own. It's not like we don't need a listening ear or a shoulder to cry on, but the trauma or the trust of not having anyone plays a big part. I can only speak for myself as I write, but it's very hard for me to trust when you have memories of deceit and disloyal people.

At the age of 35, I only have three very good friends, and I'm totally fine with that; they all play a major role in my life. My circle is very small and I like it that way. The less a person knows, the less they can hurt you. That's how I used to think. Now, I feel like I'm open to new plans and friends. I'm just selective.

Life After Better Days showed me so much. Wow! I'm learning to face my problems and find my own solutions. I don't and won't tolerate very much either. I am a work of art, I stand for a lot, and I really don't fall for anything. Even when I speak to someone and try to encourage or motivate them, the biggest thing I say is, "Life is uncomfortable, and if you continue to wait for the right time, you'll never accomplish anything. Action plus discipline is what will keep you on top. The easiest task to accomplish is complaining. Throw that fear of *what if* out and start thinking *as I know I can and I will.*

Being a writer can be discouraging, but the more you write, the more you become eager to be heard through words. Let it flow on paper. Watch how beautifully it comes out. Just let go. I'm in a race with myself. My story is not a sad story; it's a real one. It's a story of a girl who transformed into a woman who fought through a storm she thought would never end, although I still face many challenges in my life. This woman is ready for war. Risks can be dangerous, but routine can be deadly when you want to better yourself.

Comfort has killed more dreams than daring ever did. That's a fact. It starts with you! I promise. I'm not perfectly fine. Each day I feel a different way, but I'm not shattered. I'm in the process of healing, seeing beauty in tough situations, and making it a part of my journey.

I will continue to grow because when I speak to certain individuals, I hear fear, so I always try to motivate them that nothing can stop growth like fear does. A lot of us won't even take the first step toward our gift or purpose because we see only failure at the end of it.

Fear will program you to be afraid of life, and when anything drastic happens, you'll really feel like the world's over. Ask me how I know? My dad's death crushed me. It left me empty, cold, nauseous, and undefeated. I'm still grieving, but one thing he taught all of his children was to show action and never live in fear.

One thing I can say is that what separated my mother and father's parenting is that my mother taught us everything we needed to know, just in case a tragedy happens. My father went through life, unaware of the moments he was teaching us. He was our protector, so he taught us physically, and my mother taught us verbally about life.

There's so much more to life than fear, but you can't really explore anything. Fear makes you live in a bubble of uncertainty. You can either convince yourself that the fears are valid or you can shift your entire perspective and empower yourself to live through whatever life has in store for you. You'll even have to detour many times, but the joy of getting back on track is worth the reward.

Trust me, I'm living in everything I write. I also have to understand there's a difference between being strong and being powerful. I didn't write about *Life After Better Days* for me. A strong woman raised me, so I honestly want to help someone out with my trauma story.

Considering what I have been through, I have learned to manifest my power and turn what happened into a positive experience. At this stage in my life, I no longer just think of myself as a public speaker; I have to step outside my comfort zone. I'm no longer strong, I'm powerful.

↔

January 30, 2024

The Art of Detachment

I'm so emotional today. Literally everywhere, my thoughts and emotions keep crashing together, and it's uncontrollable. A funny thing about Life is that you only have a couple of minutes to let it out, and then it's back to reality. I can feel it deep down inside, but I can't let it out, maybe because I'm at work.

I woke up today and felt like life was attacking me the moment I opened my eyes. My youngest has been sick for the last couple of days, and that's a task in itself, especially when you have no support or help. I do everything by myself, and it's not because I want to; it's because when I ask for help, I don't get it, so I stopped asking. I learned to be accustomed to living without or working hard to get it. I learned the art of detachment by navigating life's situations on my own. You can only be rejected so many times before you just give up. Today was challenging, but I made it through.

-Rebirthing-

Rebirthing yourself is very personal. You have to be focused and not naive to the fact that you want more for your life. It's a therapy that helps you mentally, physically, and emotionally.

The first task you must complete is to honestly eliminate people, places, and things that have caused you pain and agony. Even if you have to dig deep into your childhood and forgive anyone who causes you to rebirth. Rebirthing hurts because, for some, they are accustomed to the normalcy of just hiding, living through, and suffering in silence. That's not healthy.

You have to be released. Your mind shouldn't have to suffer what you endured. I knew firsthand about "Just Living" until I took a step back and decided to rebirth my thoughts and life.

I wanted to overcome trauma and anxieties that stemmed from birth. *Life After Better Days* was very dark and cold, also lonely, but much needed. Rebirth to me is renewal, rejuvenation, and revival of your way of thinking and your everyday life. Taking deep breaths, inhaling and exhaling when meditating, does wonders for me.

You're engaging your soul, bringing and regaining happiness in your existence. My children are really my rebirth in human form. Every one of them serves a purpose in my life, and I remind them daily how much I appreciate and love them. Teaching them the paths they should take is a form of rebirth. What I pour into my daughters is worth every tear, every drop of blood, and every sweet moment, even the sacrifices and decisions I made to teach them that Better Days do exist.

But *Life After Better Days* may take you through some unexpected roads that you may have to take to get back on track. Life will knock you down, but getting back up and keeping trying is better than lying and drowning in your sorrows for too long. The process is worth the reward of your happiness that'll come.

I want to encourage my readers to give their souls a break; don't be so hard on yourself- your soul deserves love, too. We tend to be so busy giving everyone else love that we often overlook the love we deserve.

-Rebirth Yourself-

Get out the old way of thinking. Being in your own head is the worst. Ask me how I know again... lol! Ninety percent of the time, I'm in my own head, just thinking of ways to survive, not knowing that I'm honestly not living. Having that mindset means doing what you can at the present moment and working on what you can, but don't go into overdrive. Doing so will burn your body out.

Always stand on your two feet, even if you're wobbling. It's your time. I want to leave this earth knowing that I paved my way and inspired someone, but more importantly, knowing I rebirthed myself for the better. Even as a strong person, I encourage you to rebirth for many reasons. We get tired of pouring, riding, and giving to the world when you don't have enough strength for self.

-Reset-

I realized the moment you do reach out for a helping hand, most times, you don't even get it, because the world is so used to you always being there (and that's okay), but you have to be adequate enough to be of any assistance to anyone and not bleed on them with your problems or burdens.

Rebirth yourself again for your children; this is very important. A lot of parents are dealing with a lack of love and affection that their parents didn't show them. So, fast forward to them becoming parents, they show not one ounce of love to their children. For that very reason, I honestly believe they were not shown or even had the love they needed to pour into what they produced.

Let's dig deeper. The fact that it's not our parents' fault, rather it's a domino effect: their mothers and fathers weren't loved. Break the cycle, break the chains of generational curses. It's never too late.

Rebirth, to me, is a spiritual enlightenment that causes a person to lead a new life. You are tuned into the fact that only you can fix your life, even if you didn't cause the damage that's been done. Awake your inner self and rebirth your way into a better life. The winter of 2024 was my time to just be alone and process my thoughts. Everything was so loud around me that I couldn't hear. I was dealing with the loss of my dad, switching jobs, being at my lowest, and nobody knew.

My smile was as pretty as a picture, but my soul was cold, and I didn't care. I saw myself, and not knowing who I was, I couldn't even identify the person in the mirror.

In the midst of my storm, I lost a lot of people. Being misunderstood comes with a significant number of goodbyes. I'm still in my storm, weeping, but to acknowledge it and have the ability to go through it is step one. Reserving my life and well being is all that mattered. I require so much for myself after all I've been through. I'm at the point in my life that I want to live quietly. I love to live in the moment, just because we think it's not enough when in fact it really is.

I feel as though the majority rule is that you beat yourself up and think about *where you should be,* but the power is in the present. How do you feel right now as you read *Life After Better*

Days? The key to unlocking your breakthrough is in the HERE and NOW!

When your mind is at a constant speed of racing to look into your future, you forget to live right now. Plan for it, yes, but still live. You are not grounded; you are not anchored, and you will block the flow of your blessings. All in all, fall in love with the "NOW." Slow down for the present moment and enjoy it.

↔

After about three months since the passing of my dad, I was having panic attacks. Just picture yourself lying in bed, and your chest instantly begins to tighten. The room is dark, and all you can do is cry until it's over. Some nights, I couldn't even move to get water to drink or splash on my face or even grab my phone to call for help. To be even more honest, eighty percent of my panic attacks occurred when I was drunk and deep in my thoughts.

Now, don't get me wrong; I've always drank alcohol because I love the way it makes me feel. I cried for three months straight, just trying to process everything, on top of being a working mother and dealing with a relationship. Honestly, I don't even know how I did it, but I did. Just writing this hurts.

I then realized that death is a part of life, and of course, I'll forever grieve, but I need to change the way I look at life and own my happiness, even when I'm in disarray. I challenged the way I felt and changed my perspective. Some days are better than others, but for me to continue to heal, I've to celebrate even through death. Our dad wouldn't want us to always be sad. It's humanly impossible, but to get up every day and still strive is all that matters. Enjoy the process of pain so that you, as a person, can come out stronger.

Rebirth You!

February 5, 2025

Today was a bit tiring, simply because my weekend was filled with so much joy. Yet, I was also overwhelmed with Aa'Layah's 7th birthday.

Nevertheless, I planned on visiting my brother, who's incarcerated, and was on edge. I haven't seen my brother since 2020 due to COVID, and that's not like me. If you know, then you know! I don't make excuses when it comes to visits. I never wanted Dom to feel like he was alone in the world, so visits were a must for me.

As I was riding up to the jail, I FaceTime my mom and was talking for a couple of minutes. She said something about undergarments when visiting a person who is incarcerated. It dawned on me that I had to stop at the store to get a sports bra, knowing I should have worn one as I was getting dressed. I was disappointed in myself because I knew the rules. I stopped at the nearest Walmart and purchased a bra and was good to go.

Approaching the jail, you're stopped by two guards who search your car for damn near ten minutes, after which you go inside. I'm big on energy and vibes. It was cold as soon as I took off my coat. I mean it was a cold morning, but this cold was different. A couple of minutes later, I went in and sat down.

It took a while for my brother to come out to the visiting room, but as soon as he did, we both lit up like Christmas trees. Holding back tears was what I did. My brother has been through a lot. We all have, but his pain is a little different because we have the option to have different ways of coping, and he has none.

From my brother's killing and then our dad's passing. Talk about crushed. We dug deep into conversation, but I asked him how he felt, and he replied, "I'll grieve when I come home." Talk about crying on the inside. I could feel myself falling apart on the inside, but I held my composure.

All in all, I'm writing this to say that from start to finish, my whole morning was spent detouring and rerouting, but I got it together. Life isn't always smooth and may have bumps in the road, but ride the detour out until you get to your destination. You really don't know what a person goes through. I saw pain and fearlessness in my brother's eyes. Losing anyone while incarcerated can be tough on anyone. Love them in a time of need; it's much needed. I'm glad that he still has his sanity and strength, but he's human, too. It's the real world, no social media involved.

↔

Honestly, I often say I would love for social media to crash. It took away the genuine love that we, as people, should have and put it on a social site. I like to show people, physically, that I care and love them through actions, not just words, and that's just me. In life, you will realize what's real and fake. Some will test you, others will use you, and many will teach you, but the ones who are truly important are the ones that bring out the best in you.

-The Ending-

In all reality, there is no ending. You just keep going. My next step in life will be just that; I want to use my gift to help others in any area of their life. Even gaining the knowledge I need to keep moving is motivation in itself, especially from individuals who have or may have walked in my shoes.

Everyone's story is different, but that's the beauty in it. You won't believe I wrote *Life After Better Days* while I was hurting and in a dark place. I had a lot of time to think, process life, sit with my pain, and figure out my next move. What I realized is that I needed this season of loneliness. I never would have thought that losing my dad would change my way of thinking in a good way, but honestly, I never took my life for granted.

Being spiritually connected, I believe in certain things and don't tolerate too much. I require respect because I give respect, and nothing less. You must set high standards in life and never settle for anything less.

My main plan is to reach my full potential, so I must forgive even when I feel betrayed by the people I thought I could count on and trust! My soul is still learning to clap for the pieces of myself that nobody wants to clap for, because I suffer in silence at times.

Believe it or not, I am in the process of figuring things out on my own. I am still healing silently. I'm more focused than ever right now in my life. I want to become the best version of myself so that I can raise my daughters properly so that I won't bleed on them with my trauma, and if I did, I'm able to help them through it because I am not a perfect parent.

It's not fair to any parents who are dealing with trauma. I pray you can work on yourself. Your children are watching, and the older they get, the more they understand, and the harder it is for generational curses to break. The reason many people can't enjoy a sense of peace is that they've been in survival mode since childhood. Some do not know how to live a regular life because they're so used to chaos. Change that ASAP.

Don't let negative thinking disrupt your thought process, as your mind is always on the go. I get it; it's a defense mechanism to change that fast! Preparing for the worst because you know what it's like to have your peace shattered is the most hurtful thing ever. I know firsthand what it's like to get your hopes up only to be let down, so you now expect failure to occur. Nope...heal and let that be the end of your nervous system being in a state of dysfunction. Enjoy the moment!!

You literally become what you think about. If you want that life of peace, you have to create it. Start visualizing it daily. Remember to overcome the struggles you face by simply thinking positively. You are facing life lessons; it's all a test for your testimony and to see if you are truly committed to your life. People just talk without putting their words into action. Do you want to know what I did to ease my pain of self-sabotage? I stopped looking for closure from those who traumatized me. My closure came from forgiving (which was very hard for me).

I also chose to love myself, heal, and upgrade my boundaries, which is why I don't tolerate things very much. I've learned to raise my vibrations and turn my wounds into wisdom, stepping into my power. The time is now, and it will all change. Life is about choices and changes; making the choice to change one's life is so fleeting. Pray about whatever you need to. We are on borrowed time; nothing is more challenging than truly working on yourself, trying to break bad habits and old ways. **End the cycle!**

↔

This season has taught me a great deal, and I hope it has taught you as well. Learning to sit in your pain was the hardest thing for me, as though all I know is shadowing my pain, not being able to really feel the feeling of how I'm emotionally unbalanced, being called to go into hermit mode, or taking time for myself to go inward is needed. Mentally, physically, and emotionally!

It's time for us to pour back into ourselves. Stop letting people speak their fears into your way of thinking. Always speak highly of yourself and everything around you, even if you aren't too sure about your next move. **Speak Life!**

The ending is never here when you want to level up and do right. *Life After Better Days* wore me and my family members out. We were falling apart. With all the grieving, it was a terrible dysfunction. Arguments and people hurting people with words because they are hurt. *Life After Better Days* took me out of my zone in a trance, but I do know I will fight to the end to tell my story!

Pray about it all, we as people are too afraid or ashamed to go through stuff, and for people to know about it. I lived that way for years. This will not be me anymore. My siblings and I were so divided after the passing of our father. Death is challenging; it breaks you because, in all reality, it broke us down.

Trying to forgive each other is our downfall, but I've been praying more and more for us all because this new me just wants peace. Even in my relationship world, I require peace. It's okay to let go when you're not whole and going through life, especially when it's not something you can transfer.

Trust your instincts and know that it's okay to let go when a relationship no longer brings joy into your life. It's a tough decision, but sometimes it's the right way to go! You can't pour into someone when your cup is empty. You have to take a step back and ask yourself, "Who can pour into my cup?" It's a terrible feeling.

Stand on your two feet about you and what you are willing to allow, even if it's scary because you don't know how "a person" will react to your new boundaries. STAND YOUR GROUND! Putting yourself first is the ultimate goal, and I mean it.

Remember that if you are a good, humble, and sweet person, the devil will come after you through people. He will lead them to treat you wrong just to see if you will sink or swim away. Like I said before, do not let anyone knock you off your greatness.

Personally, I tend to attract broken individuals, whether it's friends, family relationships, coworkers, etc. I'm like a magnet to people who have dealt with life in a traumatic way. I don't even see it as a bad thing, only because I, too, was broken and currently trying to get my life back together. Being a strong, functionally depressed person, nobody can ever tell. We tend to want to help anyone, especially if love is involved.

The only difference with myself is I'm not ashamed of anything I've been through, currently going through or going to go through. It's a part of life; it will be a part of my future. It's life and I gotta live it my way, mistakes, wins, losses, good and bad seasons of MINES!!! I'll never shadow my world anymore!!

Time heals all wounds, but while it's healing, situations and life do hurt until the wound is completely healed. I'm all over the place with my life. I know what I want and what I'm capable of doing, but I just need a consistent flow to be set free from my own inner thoughts. It's like one day I'm okay, and the next day I'm not.

The process of grieving is so optimistic. Our dad was and will forever be missed. One thing I do know is that he loved his children but would be disappointed at all the arguments, fallouts, hurt, and the pain that came with his death. I can really hear him now telling us all to "SHUT UP!" LOL. I just want to one day accept the fact that he is at rest and doesn't have to worry about his children down here on Earth.

We are all adults, and his time on Earth is over. He did so much for us, and I'm sure we are all grateful. We just have to learn to live through the grieving process, even if it's therapy, whatever it takes to mend our broken hearts. If you know me on a personal level, you know I'm crying right now. But this, too, shall pass, and each awakening day is another chance to get through life. *Life After Better Days* LITERALLY BROKE ME. IT BROKE ME DOWN!!!

Life After Better Days made me realize that life must go on. You have to maneuver and pivot through life; it doesn't matter what's thrown at you. Difficult times happen to everyone, believe it or not. Don't let the world we live in today program you into thinking no one is dealing with life, trust me, we all are.

I'm an open book! That's why I'm able to shed light on my trials and tribulations so that I can help anyone in need. This is my second book, so my ultimate goal is to motivate, and my first book is to inspire someone. To cope with life, you need to learn how to deal with stress and hardships; that's where I come in. I may not have all of the answers, but I do have the experience. I will never tell you how to approach your situation, but motivating you is truly my calling.

As of this very day, even with me being a motivator, I feel sad. There are five stages of grieving, and in all honesty, I have no idea where I'm at, being in denial, angry, bargaining (meaning going through the process of what happened), depression, or if I accept it or not. Some days, I go through all five stages, and I know some of you do as well.

Not knowing or having a handbook, I resort to working, picking up extra shifts, sleeping, or writing. But if you're paying attention, it was the abuse of alcohol. It was even hard for me to be out hanging with my friends and family because I was too far gone in my thoughts. Even over loud music, my thoughts were much louder.

I promised myself, after writing and publishing *Life After Better Days*, that I would seek help for myself and my daughters. It's very much needed, but in the back of my mind, I was wondering if the therapist would understand??

Life After Better Days...

Don't I wish I knew, but the reality is that none of us ever do. Our life was already written out, and we were just letting it unfold; we have no control. Life is still happening every day. Knowing how it will all play out will enable the human body to perform optimally, but since we are not, we ultimately have to figure life out as it comes.

I can and will never stop living the *Life After Better Days*, so I will always have a story. But for now, I'm learning to love myself more, become a better mother, sister, daughter, friend, significant other, and, more importantly, a better me. Being the person I am, I recognize that I require improvement. By no means am I perfect, and neither is the person reading this book.

Do what works for you! Never give anyone from your past platform too much attention. Learn from your mistakes, no matter how big or small they may be, and even if they are part of your story. Make sure you end the chapter and somehow live with and accept the things you can't change. Life is really just all about living.

I learned that *Life After Better Days* is just about living for the moment. Losing a brother, father, and several other family members that meant the world to me during *Better Days* and *Life After Better Days* made me understand so much.

Also in My *Life After Better Days*, I lost my father's mother. To be honest, I don't know how to feel from being so numb over my father's death. I know she's at peace. After the death of her one and only son, we had several talks about him and how they didn't have the best relationship. Although she passed away from another cause of death, I believe she passed away from a broken heart. The conversations we had privately were all about hurt and the acceptance of many things.

After our father's death, I knew she wouldn't last much longer on earth. A broken heart is real, and many can't endure it. Neither could our father. He missed both of my brothers, one being incarcerated and the other one killed nine months before he died. I only speak from the heart. Some may not even agree, but when your heart is broken, it's hard to mend. You try to cope with the fact that maybe you didn't do enough or could have made life better, and it eats away at you. That's why you have to forgive yourself and heal. At least try some healing, but for others, it causes them to lose their battle, resulting in death.

Writing a second book was necessary; I gave you my world, my emotions, my thoughts, and ultimately, my life. Things will be a rollercoaster ride but be willing to fight. Even if you lose, get back up. As I close up *Life After Better Days*, I will say a prayer for me, as I do for everyone.

I'm proud of laying my life out for the world to see and understand the way I think. You may even look in the mirror and say, "Damn, Nina really read me through *Life After Better Days*."

When you express your true self, many people get offended. So what!!! The path of being true to yourself means that you look in the mirror and see what no one else can.

Life After Better Days is a book to show people what I was running from. The truth is that accountability is not something people are fond of. On the contrary, we have been conditioned to be really good at playing the blame game or just pointing fingers at someone else.

However, this makes the world fake and ignorant. Even through social media, people hide who they truly are to maintain an image. I AM ME and *Life After Better Days* were major key points of my life. Dare to be a genuine soul in this world we live in and see how far it takes you. REAL IS RARE... and all I ever wanted to do is leave a legacy for my daughters. I knew right after high school that writing was my thing. I always had a story to tell. The TRUTH... MY TRUTH.

The adrenaline I felt during this entire writing journey was both emotional and fulfilling. I have no regrets on this very day. I'm not completely complete, and maybe I never will be, but I'm different. My way of thinking, the way I live, and even how I raise my daughters are all unique. Living in a peaceful world is my goal, as I've endured so much in my life and struggled with inner turmoil. This doesn't mean my life is in disarray; it just means I'm dealing with everyday life, so whatever doesn't bring me peace and happiness has to go.

Literally, nobody tells you how hard it is to reprogram your brain so you can allow amazing things to happen and unfold after so much trauma and hurt. Try it and see; I promise you, if you do it correctly, that's just the start of your healing. Now, I'm not saying it will be easy, but start somewhere.

Better Days showed me that I am capable, but *Life After Better Days* showed me and taught me that, even after everything, I just need to keep going. To be a vessel and a public speaker, so that I can not only heal myself, but also heal others. Anything that I do on earth is for the elevation of myself and the people that I can speak life into. It's not to boost my ego, look down upon anyone, or frown upon them. Having that mindset also leads you to the realization that you can't get through to everyone, but if you can help just one person, you have done what you were called to do.

Not everyone will be my audience, and that's okay! As I mentioned earlier, everyone's story is unique. My ending to *Life After Better Days* is just to heal, meditate, and live my life. I've been through enough, just laying my life out into my second book was exhausting with so many deaths occurring during my journey. Some days, I struggled to even smile, I cried, and the list goes on. My message to my readers is to keep going even in *Life After Better Days!* Moving forward is a process! You have to have faith.

We live in a world where everything and everybody is in a rush. I had to learn to slow down. I also had to learn that there's a difference between having faith and wasting time. Faith is preparing you for what's to come. You may not see the results right away, but when you put in your footwork, you'll see growth. Wasting time is a whole different thing. Don't sit and waste time on anything.

Here's the breakdown: The pressure of life will put you in situations where you feel like you should put in work, and when you reevaluate your life, you'll live in line with your purpose. It'll remove what doesn't belong! Trust me, I know.

Real purpose comes with a cost; it's like a gamble. Purpose will have you digging deep within yourself so that it can reveal who you are. After you figure that out, you can be drawn to certain people, places, and things. Without purpose, you'll never be able to move forward.

You also need to develop empathy for yourself. Living in your purpose also develops maturity. It keeps you still, even when you want to make a drastic decision, even when life is still moving. It's shaping you to walk in your purpose.

Life After Better Days has been amazing yet painful, to say the least. But my first step into healing is to take baby steps and pray for my mind, sanity, and strength. I always knew my words would get me far. I knew that I could help someone. Hear me when I write this: just trust that there's a reward on the other side. Don't fall into regret.

Keep working on making the decision, even if it's baby steps! Ultimately, you get what you give out. So at least try... . It's not life that's holding you back from healing or growing; it's YOU. If you recognize areas in your life that need improvement, work on them for your own benefit so that you can become a better person.

Keep fighting; you have two options: you can give up or get beaten down by life and not live for your purpose. The ambitious mindset is lethal. Separate yourself from the crowd and get uncomfortable. Even if you can be one percent better than you were yesterday, you've made progress.

PAIN- Physical suffering or discomfort: *FIX IT.*

PAST- Going back in time and no longer existing as a part of a person's history.

PURPOSE- The reason for which something is done or created; an intention to aim for a reason for doing something or for allowing something to happen.

Keep all this in mind. I did just that. I'm trying to create my own happiness with the life that was presented to me. I'm not ashamed or embarrassed; I don't care who judges me. It's my life. I wouldn't dare feel scared for anyone to read this book! I love myself. After reading *Life After Better Days*, I pray that you would grow your pain, your past, and live in your purpose, and keep your feet moving. It definitely gets greater with time.

↔

Ending Poem

As **Life After Better Days** *came to an end, tears flowed, and my heart definitely did several back bends.*

Sleepless nights all in my thoughts, wondering why I was chosen to deal with situations, but I fought.

Coming to the conclusion, making amends, and knocking down barrels of hurt, pain, and sin.

I sat in my emotions, screaming, crying, even silently some days.

Just take the first step.

Be strong in each hour, carry on your story, and be proud of your power.

You could have given up, but instead, you chose to fight. Battling the dark days so that you can see the light.

You're the author of your life.

If you can't cope, don't put a full stop on it. Battle through it with so much hope.

Whether you lose or win as a person, we will withstand stress and anxiety; we will conquer and command.

It's time to live and give it all you got. At the end of the tunnel, you'll see why giving up wasn't all you got. The ending is just a beautiful beginning.

And if you read **Life After Better Days**, *you will see a girl who did so many things, then you'll see a woman blossoming.*

Through tragedy and upbringings, the end's not near, so keep moving, not giving up or living in fear.

Life keeps going even if you don't want it to...

Be the reason why someone can finally take control of their situation, with no regrets, and have reciprocation.

The ending is not over; it's just memories that never mend.

For they are puzzle pieces of all the things that you had to end.

Life After Better Days

Nina